"Honey, let go of Mr. Holden," Annie said to her nephew.

Bright eyes beamed back at her. "But, Aunt Annie, I've been waiting for-*evvv*-er."

She smiled and gently tugged the little boy's arm away from Colt's leg. Looking up, her gaze locked once more with Colt's alarmed brown eyes.

Ever since she'd found the letter that revealed who Leo's daddy was, God had laid a heavy burden on her heart. It had taken her house burning down to make her figure out what she wanted to do. And that was to come find out what kind of man Colt was.

She'd been here all of ten minutes and things weren't looking so good. "I'm sorry about this. I guess I should introduce myself. I'm Annie Ridgeway, and this is my nephew, Leo."

"Our house burned down and my room is gone," Leo said, staring up at Colt.

Colt's browr house burn

She didn't r in his reaction.

So the man does have a heart buried in there somewhere.

Books by Debra Clopton

Love Inspired

*The Trouble with Lacy Brown
*And Baby Makes Five
*No Place Like Home
*Dream a Little Dream
*Meeting Her Match
*Operation: Married by Christmas
*Next Door Daddy
*Her Baby Dreams
*The Cowboy Takes a Bride
*Texas Ranger Dad
*Small-Town Brides
  "A Mule Hollow Match"

*Lone Star Cinderella
*His Cowgirl Bride
†Her Forever Cowboy
†Cowboy for Keeps
  Yukon Cowboy
†Yuletide Cowboy
*Small-Town Moms
  "A Mother for Mule Hollow"
**Her Rodeo Cowboy
**Her Lone Star Cowboy
**Her Homecoming Cowboy

*Mule Hollow
†Men of Mule Hollow
**Mule Hollow Homecoming

DEBRA CLOPTON

First published in 2005, Debra Clopton is an award-winning, multi-published novelist who has won a Booksellers Best Award, an Inspirational Readers' Choice Award, a Golden Quill, the *Cataromance* Reviewers' Choice Award, *RT Book Reviews* Book of the Year, and Harlequin.com's Readers' Choice Award. She was also a 2004 finalist in the prestigious RWA Golden Heart, a triple finalist in the American Christian Fiction Writers Carol Award and most recently a finalist in the 2011 Gayle Wilson Award for Excellence.

Married for 22 blessed years to her high school sweetheart, Wayne Clopton, Debra was widowed in 2003. Happily, in 2008, a couple of friends played matchmaker and set her up on a blind date with Chuck Parks. Instantly hitting it off, Debra and Chuck were married in 2010. They live in the country with Chuck's two high-school-age sons. Debra has two adult sons, a lovely daughter-in-law and beautiful granddaughter—life is good! Her greatest awards are her family and spending time with them. You can reach Debra at P.O. Box 1125, Madisonville, TX 77864 or at debraclopton.com.

Her Homecoming Cowboy

Debra Clopton

Love Inspired

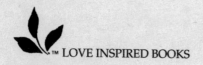

™ LOVE INSPIRED BOOKS

Recycling programs
for this product may
not exist in your area.

ISBN-13: 978-0-373-87759-1

HER HOMECOMING COWBOY

Copyright © 2012 by Debra Clopton

www.LoveInspiredBooks.com

Printed in U.S.A.

There is a season for everything,
and a time for every activity under heaven.
—*Ecclesiastes* 3:1

This book is dedicated to my good friends
Melanie Trant and Joanna Harris...
your hearts of gold and sassy attitudes made me
fans from the first moments we met! As they say in
Texas, God did *"real good"* when He ran our paths
together. Thanks for being my friends.

Chapter One

"Well, hi there, Colt Holden, bull rider extraordinaire. My goodness you're breathtaking to watch on a bull.... Oh, and by the way, I'm here to tell you that you're a daddy!"

Annie Ridgeway recited the words in her head. Nope, that was certainly not the way to break the news. Though humor did lighten up a hard situation most times, in this case...not so much.

Annie and her sister, Jennifer, had always had very different ideas about life. Following rodeos around and being too friendly with the cowboys who rode bulls and broncs had been, in Annie's view, a terrible thing. Then again, she and her sister had always been opposites. Jennifer thought Annie was a stick-in-the-mud, and she thought Jennifer was a...well, to put it bluntly, a *lot* too loose with her affections.

The two sisters had basically disagreed about almost everything right up until the day Jennifer died a year ago.

They had disagreed about everything, that is, but their love for Leo. On loving Leo they had agreed completely.

What was best for Leo—on that they'd remained consistent—disagreeing till the very end.

Annie started over. *"Mr. Holden, you don't know this, but you are the daddy of my six-year-old nephew, Leo. Surprise!"*

Groaning, she bit her lip and nibbled on that straight-forward approach. It was blunt. But it was the truth.

Six years. That was a long time to keep something as important as this hidden. Whether the rowdy cowboy had wanted to know or not, he should have been told.

That ended today.

Annie had decided today was the last day she was going to be responsible for such a significant piece of her nephew's life. Having made this monumental deci-sion hadn't made it easy for her. Oh, no. She'd be lying if she claimed that. It had been down-right hard; in fact, God had actually gotten a little rough with her to get her attention!

She tried *again* to squelch the need to turn and run. Dread so heavy she could barely breathe settled over her as she pulled her old clunker onto the gravel drive of the Holden Ranch. Squinting against the bright July sunshine, she battled with where to go—the house or the office. The small metal office sat closer to the road and had three trucks sitting in front of it, making it the logical choice.

Continuing to nibble at her lip she studied the simple office building of the Holden Ranch, and then the white ranch house in the distance. The sense of dread wrapped tighter around her, suffocating her…

You have nowhere else to go.

Ha! She could find a way to make it—

This is for Leo.

She closed her eyes.

Everything was for her little Leo.

"Is this where *he* lives?"

Leo's question interrupted her thoughts. Pulling herself together, Annie turned to look at her six-year-old nephew. He was sitting in his safety chair in the backseat of the car, beaming with expectations that terrified her.

What if this guy was a jerk?

Even though Leo thought they were going to meet Colt Holden, the man he most admired in all the world, Leo had no idea what this meeting meant to his future.

Forcing a smile and ignoring the rolling of her stomach, she answered, "Yes, I believe it is. This is a great day, isn't it?" Sick as she felt she couldn't help being excited for Leo—after all, he was meeting his hero today.

He idolized pro-bull rider Colt Holden. Up until her death a year ago, her sister had told Leo all kinds of bedtime stories about the bull rider. They watched him when he was on television competing in pro-bull-riding events. And Jennifer had posted pictures of Colt Holden all over Leo's room.

Annie's mind filled with images of the bull rider's dazzling smile in many poses and his gritty concentration when he was riding the fierce bulls.

There was no denying that the cowboy was awe-inspiring in that regard. And no wonder that Leo, clueless about who his father was, had grown up adoring the cowboy his mother had painted as the most wonderful man in the world. This should have given Annie a little heads-up on the matter. But it hadn't.

Whether the man was wonderful, she wasn't so sure. Even if he was a good man, he'd have a lot to live up to.

"Annie Aunt, is this where he lives?" Leo asked, using the backward term of affection that he'd called her all his life.

"Yes. At least I think so. He's going to be surprised when he meets you and finds out how much you know about him."

He beamed proudly at her. "He's the greatest bull rider in the *whole* wide world. He ain't won the championship 'cause he always gets a bad draw on his bulls out there at the big national rodeo."

She wasn't sure about all of that, and really had no idea why the cowboy had never won the championship the five times he'd made the nationals.

The man was elite in his field whether he had or hadn't. "You amaze me, Leo. I can tell you this—that's one lucky cowboy to have you so crazy about him."

Leo's face twisted into a huge smile. "I'm so excited I could whoop!" he exclaimed, and proceeded to do exactly that by exploding with a loud *whoop.* "Gosh, Annie Aunt, it's gonna be great!" Rocking his safety seat in his enthusiasm, he said, "He's gonna like me. And since we're gonna live in the same town, I bet he'll teach me to ride bulls and rope—maybe even how to fish."

Annie's mouth went dry and the slow burn of indigestion spread across her chest. Leo's expectations as a fan were huge. How would Colt Holden react to a little-boy fan, so infatuated with him?

Most important—how would he react when he knew he had a son?

* * *

Colt Holden stared at his brothers. They meant well, but right now the last thing he needed was their sympathy. Or their mothering.

"You aren't sleeping at night." Luke, his oldest brother, challenged him. The words echoed off the thick wooden paneling of the office and also Colt's equally thick bad disposition. He scowled.

"I never said that. If this is some sort of intervention, you fellas need to back up."

"Come on, Colt." Jess, two years older than him, rammed a hand through his dark hair, worry in his blue eyes. "Have you looked in a mirror lately? You haven't slept since the wreck. You've lost at least ten pounds, too. You've holed up out there and haven't come away from the cabin since you got home."

"You look bad on the outside and we're afraid you look worse on the inside," Luke finished. His brown eyes, so much like Colt's, were solemn.

Colt rubbed the stubble on his chin with his good hand. He didn't need to look in a mirror to know what he looked like. These days the less he looked in a mirror the better off he was. The contempt he felt for himself was almost too much to bear. And this sympathy—intervention—*whatever* you called it, wasn't helping.

"You've got to rein this in," Luke continued. "You've got to move forward."

"Move *forward.*" Black emotion swept through Colt. "If this is what y'all called me about this morning, then I'll be cuttin' you loose. I just want to be left alone."

"We get that," Luke offered, his voice gentling. "But you have to pull yourself out of this hole you're in. This isn't going to bring anyone back or change what happened in that car wreck."

"It wasn't your fault," Jess finished.

"That doesn't help me sleep at night," Colt growled. He was six years younger than Luke and two years younger than Jess. Since he was eight, when his mother left them and their home fell apart, his older brothers had been his heroes. They'd been the ones who'd provided for him and looked out for him when their parents hadn't. They'd protected him as much as they could and offered as much love as two boys their age could offer. But he was all grown up now, and they couldn't help him. No one could.

He wasn't so sure God could help him at this point.

"You have to figure out a way past it," Luke said. "Give it to God."

Colt bolted straight out of the chair; every muscle in his strained back protested while his broken collarbone shot fire through him. It was pain he welcomed—pain he deserved.

Memories, like firebrands, seared into his soul. "Fellas, I can't do this. Not now." He headed for the door, escape all he could think about. Hell on earth had nothing on what he felt. Jess slid into his path as Luke came around the edge of the desk and flanked him.

"We talked with a specialist," Luke said. "And he suggested some counseling—"

"I'm not—" Colt stared at his brothers. "I don't need some guy with a Ph.D telling me I need to get over it." He gritted the words out. They blew up like fireworks. "Do you think the family I wiped out cares whether I 'get over it.' No. They wish I'd had my head on straight that night. They wish I'd have pulled over ten minutes earlier when I realized I was drifting in and out of sleep while my boot remained hard and heavy on the gas pedal!"

"Colt—" Luke tried to break in but Colt cut him off.

"And how about their loved ones? They wish I'd have been off the road where I belonged when the family they loved—" He couldn't voice it again. Couldn't look it in the face again—why couldn't his brothers get that? Some things just cut too deep.

His head pounding, he started for the door. Jess didn't move. "Colt, we're worried about you."

He looked from one brother to the other. "Don't y'all get it? Y'all can't fix this. Nothing can."

Luke laid his hand on Colt's arm. "God can."

Like a jagged blade, the words cut deep and ragged. Colt yanked his arm free. "I'd say it's a little too late for that." Two weeks ago he'd been racking up the points to compete in the National Finals Rodeo in Las Vegas in December. He'd been hauling hard across the country from rodeo to rodeo, maintaining his position as a top contender in the finals rodeo. He'd been road weary the night the drunk had swerved into him, sending him into the oncoming traffic, where his truck had hit a vehicle head-on…. Even thinking about it drove him crazy. And plunged him deeper into the murky pit he was in.

Stepping around Luke, he pushed violently on the door. It slammed open, banging against the building as it hit full force. Colt stormed outside onto the porch, fully intent on getting back to his isolated cabin, tucked into the woods at the back of their ranch.

Barreling down the steps, running as much from his thoughts as his brothers, he almost ran into the woman standing at the bottom of the steps. If she hadn't stepped back, he would have taken her out.

"I'm sorry," he blurted, coming up short. "I didn't see you."

"It's okay," she assured him, studying him intently with wide eyes that looked pale lavender in the glaring sunlight. She moved her warm blond hair behind her ear and caught her breath. He'd obviously scared her. She was rail thin, and her clothes hung on her as if they were someone else's.

Luke and Jess stepped up behind him on the porch, and her gaze flitted from him to each of them before landing back on him.

Colt stiffened, going on alert as wariness curled into a ball in the pit of his stomach. He'd learned over the last three weeks that when someone studied him like this, it wasn't a good thing.

"Hi," Luke said, taking control of the situation. "I'm Luke Holden. These are my brothers—Jess, and the guy who almost ran you over is Colt. What can we do for you?"

"Well, I'm looking for…" She paused, her gaze probing his. "You're Colt Holden. The bull rider?" she asked, as if she wasn't sure from the way he looked.

Colt rubbed his three-day-old beard. Did he look that bad? He glanced down at himself. His own jeans hung loosely on his hips, showing that Jess was right—he had lost weight. And it didn't take a look in the mirror for him to know he looked older and drawn. He felt every bit of it.

He needed to get out of here, but for the life of him, Colt couldn't tear his eyes from the woman's pale eyes.

Something stirred inside his chest at the way they searched his face, as if she were trying to look inside his head—which was not a good place for anyone to be searching right now.

"Do I know you?" Something pricked in the back of his memory. He'd feared at first that she might be a reporter. He'd learned the hard way that reporters could look innocent, too, and be as deadly as sharks.

"Um, no," she replied quickly. "We've never met. I..." She swallowed hard, then took a halting breath as her gaze hit the ground before bouncing back to his.

Was she lying? Her body language wasn't giving him any confidence in her words.

"I've actually brought my nephew to meet you. He's your number one fan. I'm sorry to intrude, but I was wondering if you would take a moment to meet him."

A *child*. Colt's heart jerked at the thought and he shook his head. "I can't— I mean, I'm not—"

Behind her, the creak of the battered blue car's door opening drew his attention. His heart sank as a little boy, about five or six years old, peeked out. Colt steeled himself against the slash of guilt that ripped straight through him.

"Colt!" The kid's big eyes, wide and dancing with excitement, stared at Colt as if he was some kind of superstar. "It is you!" the kid yelled and charged.

Stepping back, Colt wanted to turn and run the other way, but he held his position, glaring at the lady. Her mouth was hanging open as the kid skidded to a halt in front of him, gravel crunching as he came.

"I been waitin' my whole long life to meet you," he

exclaimed, then joyfully threw his arms around Colt's knees.

Images of another child flashed through Colt's thoughts, breaking his heart once again into shattered pieces. Sweat popped across his brow and his heart thundered. It was all he could do to hold his ground as his gaze flew from the boy's ecstatic, upturned face, then back to the woman. To his disbelief, she looked more terrified than he felt.

Three weeks ago, Colt would have patted the kid on the head and asked him questions, drawn him into a conversation and tried to make a good impression on the boy. Today he couldn't breathe, his voice clogged in his throat and all he could think about was getting away. Life had changed in the blink of an eye. One minute he'd been on top of the world, chasing the dream reflected in this little boy's eyes. Today that dream meant nothing compared to the lives lost because of him. How did he move on from that?

How did he deserve to move forward from a tragedy that he could have prevented?

That was the question he was wrestling with.

Looking into the little boy's eyes, all Colt could think of was getting away.

Far, far away.

Chapter Two

Leo, Leo, Leo. Annie's heart tugged at his childish adoration. It was obvious Colt Holden was not used to being fawned over by kids. This shocked her. The man was a rodeo hero and there were always photos of him grinning and signing autographs... *Please tell me he is not one of those "fake it for the camera" guys.*

If he was, she might as well turn her car around and head back home. Why, the man looked terrified...and totally worn out. Deep weariness etched his face.

She was startled by his overall appearance when he'd come barreling out of the office looking fierce and scraggly. He needed a shave and two weeks of sleep.

Very different from the photos Jennifer had hung in Leo's room. Those were of a very clean-cut, slick-shaven cowboy with an intriguing glint in his eyes and mischief in his expression. This cowboy looked ten years older than the twenty-eight she knew him to be...still unbelievably handsome despite the hair that brushed his collar and the scraggly two- or three-day-old beard.

Getting over her shock, Annie bent to one knee and reached for Leo. His innocent face was a storybook of happiness as he clung to Colt Holden's legs. He was six and had never latched on to anyone like Colt. Then again, this was a dream come true for him. A dream that was looking as if it had all the potential in the world of blowing up in her face.

The enormity of what she was here to do hit her with new force, and instantly fear for Leo gripped her.

She was a take-control kinda gal. The fact that she'd procrastinated this move for a year showed her fear and worry. It had finally taken a major Godly shove and a hard dose of reality to get her moving. She'd decided to take the bull by the horns, and here she was…feeling really stupid for bringing this child here before she'd checked the man out.

"Honey, let go of—let go of Mr. Holden."

Bright eyes beamed back at her. "But, Annie Aunt, I've been waiting for-*evvv*-er."

"Yes, I know." She smiled, feeling a sense of urgency to extricate him as she gently took his arm and tugged him away. Looking up, her gaze locked once more with Colt's alarmed brown eyes.

Annie's heart sank. Ever since she'd learned who Leo's daddy was God had laid a heavy burden on her heart. It had taken her house burning down to make her figure out what she wanted to do. And that was to come find out what kind of man Colt was.

Did any honor exist beneath that facade?

She'd been here all of ten minutes and things weren't looking so good. She pushed on, though. "I'm sorry about this. I guess I should introduce myself. I'm Annie Ridgeway and this is my nephew, Leo."

"Our house burned down and my room is gone," Leo

said, staring up at Colt with big, bright stars in his eyes. "But Annie Aunt told me we were moving here to *your* town and I didn't even care anymore." He cocked his head to the side. "Does Mule Hollow have a bunch of mules?" Prone to ask random questions, it was one of many more to come.

Colt's brows crinkled in dismay. "Y-your house burned down?"

His words were choked and she didn't miss the flash of compassion in his reaction. *So the man did have a heart buried in there somewhere,* Annie thought with a smidge of relief.

Always ready to tell a story, Leo placed his hands on his hips, cocked his little blond head to the side and studied his hero even more intently—if that were even possible. "My Annie Aunt always says life kicks you in the pants sometimes. But you just gotta go with the punches." He was as serious as a little old man and she could have pinched his sweet cheeks!

"How old did you say you were?" Luke Holden asked, clearly impressed.

"I'm six. Annie Aunt says I came into the world as a twenty-year-old—and that's real old. I already lost a tooth and everything. See." He grinned and showed off his missing tooth.

That got a chuckle from Luke and Jess. Even Colt's lip quirked upward on one side.

"That's terrible," he said, his gaze sliding to her. "You lost your home."

There was something missing in the depths of his eyes. It was as if she were looking at a lake, a totally still lake with no ripples in sight. Butterflies fluttered in the pit of her stomach.

"Yes," she offered. More than intrigued by the man, she wasn't willing to accept that her pulse had actually increased as those soulful brown eyes held hers. She wanted to add more, speak intelligently; however, nothing came out.

"That's terrible for you and all the others who lost their homes," Colt continued. "We've been lucky here to have had only a few small grass fires that were caught early."

Jess, who'd seemed content to listen as he studied his brother, added, "Those fires near Austin have been rough. Not as bad as the Bastrop and Montgomery fires last year, thankfully, still bad enough. Right, Colt?" he asked, and it sounded all the world to Annie like the man was trying to keep his brother involved in the conversation.

"We didn't lose any lives in our fires," Colt said again, quietly. His brows bunched and he glanced away, toward his truck. Even took a step toward it as if impatient to get away.

It hit her then that he'd been hurrying to leave when he'd barreled from the building. "I'm sorry," she said, meaning it. "We're keeping you from something."

"No," Luke and Jess barked at the same time.

"Don't go," Leo said, tugging at Colt's pants, causing Colt to halt midstep.

"I need to get out of here. I'm sorry." He looked down at Leo, and Annie's heart tugged ruthlessly, stealing her breath with the sharpness of it.

"You can hang on a few more minutes, Colt. Can't

you?" Luke asked, clamping a hand on Colt's shoulder and squeezing.

Her gaze latched on to that hand—was Luke squeezing extra hard on Colt's shoulder?

"Yeah. Sure." Colt hit his brother with sharp eyes.

Call her late to the dance—there was definitely something churning beneath the surface here.

"I need to get back to my place." His words were quiet. And in that quietness she heard a very firm edge that was as clear as a heavy steel door slamming shut. Luke's jaw hardened as he held his peace. He didn't say anything more about Colt sticking around.

Uncertainty crashed into Annie with equal force. How would he react to the news that she'd come here to share with him? It would take more than this off-the-cuff meeting before she made her decision.

That was for certain.

"What brought you to Mule Hollow?" Luke asked, directing his questions at her, as if that would keep Colt from leaving. "I know it's not just to see my bullheaded brother."

Oh, if he only knew. "Actually, we were looking for a change. And I realized since my job at the landscaping business had burned up in the fire right along with our home, there was nothing holding us there any longer—"

"She decided it was time to make a fresh start," Leo said, grinning, as if reciting her very words. Words he'd heard her say more than just a few times.

Annie tousled his hair. "Right, I needed to find a new job and I knew if I started one there, I might never get up the nerve to relocate us."

Or the courage to tell you the truth.

Her plans for how to break the news to Colt rattled through her brain—all unusable. She'd forced herself to do this because it was probably the right thing to do, understanding that only time would tell if that were true. And also because Leo might need his daddy someday. A flashback of being trapped inside a burning building reminded her all too vividly of when she'd had that epiphany.

Pulling her thoughts away from those less pleasant ones, she saw Leo grinning up at Colt. He was rocking back and forth on his little cowboy boots as his eyes, so full of adoration, drank in his hero.

"Annie Aunt said we was coming on an adventure. I like adventures a lot. My momma used to tell me lots of stories about having adventures on bull riding and bronc bustin' and rodeo'n." He grinned wider at Colt. "You were always in the stories!"

Colt looked shocked, or as shocked as a man who was showing little emotion could look.

"You'll have to come out here and ride horses. Isn't that right, Colt?" Luke nudged Colt with his elbow when the man said nothing.

For a minute Colt looked like he was going to say something, but instead he reached for his door, wrenched it open and climbed inside the cab of his truck.

How rude—right in the middle of a conversation, the man was just going to drive off! And, he'd barely acknowledged Leo. For them to have come so far and for Leo to be so excited about seeing Colt, she knew this was going to hurt.

Just when she thought it was over and done, Colt looked down at Leo from his open window. "Hey, kid.

I...I have to go. But take this." He pulled the stiff blue rope from his truck. It had a loop on one end, and Annie recognized it was the kind used for roping steers.

"Do you like to rope?" he asked, causing Leo's eyes to grow wide.

"I ain't never done it before. Can I try?"

Colt handed Leo the rope. "Sure you can. Practice with this—it's yours."

"Thanks," Leo gushed, his voice soft with awe, drawing the word out for a mile as he studied his gift.

Colt was backing out of the driveway before Leo got the entire word out. Annie was speechless.

"Colt, wait," Luke called after him. But it was too late.

The cowboy was gone.

"Did you see what Colt gave me, Annie Aunt? Did you see what Colt gave me?"

"Isn't that something?" Annie managed, totally and completely perplexed by the cowboy driving off into the midday horizon. What in the world had just happened?

Thank goodness Leo's infatuation with Colt and the gift he'd been given distracted him.

Luke bent down and held out his hand to his nephew. Annie held her breath as Leo stopped trying to make the loop go around and shook Luke's hand.

"You want me to show you how to hold that rope?"

"Sure. Are you a bull rider, too?" Leo asked, letting Luke position his small hands on the rope. "Or a roper?"

Jess laughed, stepping into the conversation. "Are you kidding? Luke couldn't hit the broad side of a barn with a rope."

Instead of getting mad, Luke's mouth twisted into a

wide grin. "Don't listen to him. He and Colt are the better ones with the rope in the family, but ask them who taught them."

Annie smiled, relaxing a little. Liking the kindness she sensed in these two men. They were teasing each other to smooth over the actions of their brother. Little did they know they were talking to their nephew. Hope kindled anew in her heart that she was doing the right thing.

Leo looked at Jess. "Who taught you?" he asked as Luke had suggested.

A teasing grin spread across Jess's face. "My big brother, Luke. See, at one time when I was a little kid like you, I thought Luke was the best roper around. Then he taught me and Colt how to do it, and we found out just how bad he is at landing a loop. But he's a real good teacher."

Leo turned back to a smiling Luke. "Did you teach Colt to ride bulls, too? He's the best there is, and I want him to teach me how to ride a bull."

Nervous at all Leo had said, Annie realized she'd come without a well-thought-out plan of action and now she had to fess up. Before she could say anything, Jess spoke to Leo.

"I'm sorry about the fire, little buddy. But a bull busted Colt's collarbone a couple of weeks ago, so he won't be throwing a loop anytime soon. I bet when he's all healed up, you could talk him into it, though."

"Puppies!" Leo exclaimed, suddenly distracted when he spied two small puppies that came around the back of the office building, tumbling around as they wrestled together. Leo raced over to play, leaving Annie alone with the two brothers. They watched Leo fall to his knees and welcome the puppies into his lap. Both brothers had quizzical expressions as they studied Leo. When they turned almost as one to face her, Annie felt the weight of their gazes. An odd sense of guilt overcame her.

"That was good timing," Luke said. "Is there something we can do for you? Anything we need to know?"

Annie's heart hiccuped. *That he's your nephew.*

"Yeah," Jess added, an odd light in his eyes. "You came out here to see Colt. Was there a reason for that? Other than him being Leo's…hero? Maybe something we can help with?"

The weirdest feeling overcame Annie—they knew. She shook it off as guilt making her paranoid as she contemplated her dilemma. She had no one to confide her problems to or to ask advice from other than her best friend back home who had urged her to leave Leo's life as it was when Annie had confided that she was thinking of locating the boy's dad.

Looking at Leo's uncles, she told herself they didn't know anything. Her imagination was playing tricks on her. Paranoia was setting in. Finally, realizing they were waiting on a response, she asked, "Can you tell me how to get to the veterinary clinic? I'm their new office manager."

Jess snapped his fingers. "Oh, yeah—that's why your name sounded familiar," he said, his lip hitching into a lopsided smile. "My fiancée, Gabi Newberry, is the vet tech there. I knew they were expecting someone. We've had so much going on, it slipped by me that it was this week you were supposed to arrive."

She was going to be working with Colt's soon-to-be

sister-in-law.... "Oh, really," she said, hiding her surprise. "I talked to Gabi last week. I'm excited about working with her."

After a few minutes spent talking about the clinic, Annie called Leo over and they headed to the clinic using the directions Jess had given her. The clinic was right down the road from the Holden Ranch.

Annie glanced in her side-view mirror at Leo's uncles as she drove away. She wasn't sure whether she was going to break her news or not—only time would tell. She was here, though, and she had to admit that she liked the brothers very much. But the jury was still out on Colt Holden.

Annie, and Annie alone, would decide if Colt was worthy of being Leo's daddy—or if he would forever remain Leo's rodeo hero.

Chapter Three

"We are going to make this last rodeo the best one yet," a spunky-looking redhead declared as Annie and Leo entered the Mule Hollow Veterinary Clinic.

With her flaming-red hair contrasting against the tangerine capri pants and sunshine-yellow top, to say that she was bright would have been an understatement.

All four women in the room turned to look at them as Annie pulled the door shut behind her. Two other women who looked to be in their sixties, like the sunny redhead, stood in the waiting area.

One was a stout woman in a blue plaid shirt and a pair of denim overalls. Her short gray hair was the color of steel wool and just as coarse. She had a smile as wide as a half-moon, and the twinkle in her eyes was as bright as the Milky Way. Beside her stood a small-framed woman with noticeably blue eyes that contrasted with her snow-white hair, cut short and fringed around her face, and those amazing sapphire eyes. Looking at her, Annie felt immediately warm and welcome, even though she hadn't said a word yet, just smiled.

Behind the reception desk was a woman in her late

twenties. She wore her dark hair in a thick ponytail that had fallen across her left shoulder and hung over her heart. Annie assumed this was Gabi, Jess's fiancée.

Before Gabi could say anything, everyone began greeting her and Leo at the same time. Mule Hollow, Texas, was known for its matchmakers, because of an ongoing syndicated newspaper column about the little town that had gone from a dusty, dying town to a thriving place. All because of a Wives Wanted ad. Annie knew instantly that she was looking at the matchmakers, better known as the matchmaking posse. The very idea sent a startled thrill of pleasure racing through her. Not that she was looking to be matched up. More like it was neat to actually see the ladies in person.

"Hello," the redhead cooed, rushing forward and bending over to hold out her hand to Leo. There was no mistaking that this was Esther Mae Wilcox. "Aren't you a handsome little fella!"

"Howdy," the stout woman in overalls boomed, instantly bringing her larger-than-life personality off the page of the newspaper column. This had to be ranch woman Norma Sue Jenkins. "Now, Esther Mae, don't go scaring the child before we find out what his name is."

"I'm Leo. And I'm not scared," Leo declared—the kid never met a stranger. He beamed up at the ladies while they chuckled at his bright-eyed declaration.

"You must be Annie, our new office manager," the younger woman said, coming from behind the counter and holding her hand out to Annie. "I'm Gabi Newberry, the vet-tech-slash-receptionist up until now. I am *so* glad to see you."

She hadn't known how much trepidation she was feeling until this moment. The weeks of worrying over the choices she'd made and the weeks of praying, coupled with the fear that God wasn't listening to her, disappeared as she felt the warm welcome of these four ladies. Relief washed over her. She had fears about what would happen with Colt, but this was going to be all right. Leo was going to thrive in this environment if all the folks of Mule Hollow were this caring.

"I'm so glad to be here," she said, smiling.

The small lady's dainty hands clasped Annie's. "We are so glad you've come. I'm Adela Ledbetter Green, Gabi's grandmother," she said, confirming Annie's thoughts on who the delicate, kind-looking woman was.

"And I'm Esther Mae Wilcox," the redhead gushed. Then Norma Sue introduced herself.

"We are always glad to see new folks move to town," Norma Sue added. "You've rented Lilly Wells's old home, right? We call it the Tipps place because that was her maiden name and her family owned it for years."

"Yes. We're on our way out there now. We just stopped in to let the clinic know we made it to town. And that I'd be at work in the morning."

"And I'm going to go see my new day care," Leo declared before Annie could mention that they'd met Jess. "I'm six. I get to start first grade this year." Leo beamed.

"That sounds like some fine apples. You two will have to come to the rodeo we're having in town next week," Norma Sue said. "I know Leo would really enjoy it."

"I *sure* would. Is Colt Holden gonna ride bulls?"

The minute the question was out, everyone's ears perked up—or was it Annie's imagination?

"You know Colt?" They all asked, sounding like

echoes of each other. It was definitely *not* her imagination.

"Sure I do. He's the best bull rider in all of the *whole* world. And that's big, you know."

"Leo's—" Annie stopped herself just before blurting out that Leo's mother was a big fan. "Leo loves rodeo. And he is particularly a fan of Colt's. I, um, took him out there to their ranch earlier, taking a chance that he might be in town."

"How wonderful," Esther Mae exclaimed, her gaze flicking from Gabi to Norma Sue, a grin spread across her face.

"I'm engaged to Colt's brother, Jess," Gabi offered. "Were they out there?"

"Yes, they were there and Jess told me you worked here. He gave me directions."

Norma Sue planted her hands on her hips. "Was Colt there?"

"Yes, he was."

"Colt gave me a rope," Leo said proudly. "Can I go get it?"

"Sure, but stay right beside the office," she said, glad for him to have something to occupy his time.

"That was nice of Colt to give Leo a rope," Adela said, her blue eyes warm. "I'm glad he was there. I'm sure he enjoyed meeting a fan, especially one so cute."

Thinking about his odd behavior, Annie wasn't so sure about that.

"I know Leo enjoyed meeting him," she said truthfully.

"Didn't you tell Susan that you're renting the Tipps place?" Gabi asked, referring to Annie's new boss.

"Yes, we're on our way out there now. I'm just so thrilled to have found it to rent."

The ladies discussed the fact that the house was furnished, and it was out in the boondocks, down a dirt road with only one other home on the road, which belonged to Annie's new landlords, Lilly and Cort Wells.

Soon the matchmaking posse left, and to Annie's relief there had been no questions about whether she was looking for love. Annie was a little surprised by that, since the ladies were known to be fairly heavy-handed. Goodness, they were so good at what they did that it was one reason the town was flourishing. Annie figured if one day she did get a wild hair to look for a husband, then she'd come to exactly the right place. Not that that was in her foreseeable future. She had more pressing things to consider and no time to even contemplate romance.

She had Leo to think about. And that was all she had time to focus on right now.

Driving toward their new home, Annie was excited about her job. Susan had been out vaccinating a herd of cattle, and Gabi had said Annie would meet her tomorrow. Gabi said with Annie taking care of the office, it would be so much easier for her to go and assist Susan on vet calls. It was obvious that Gabi preferred being out in the field to sitting behind the desk.

Annie was excited about the people she'd met, and, despite her worries about Colt Holden and what she was going to do about Leo's situation, she had a very good feeling about Mule Hollow. The posse had been so helpful and so encouraging. And they'd really been thrilled that she was renting Lilly Wells's place.

It sounded a little secluded but nice, with plenty of wide-open space for Leo to run and play. She couldn't wait to see it.

She was certain she and Leo were going to love it.

Annie stood on the back porch of her new home the following morning and could honestly not believe her good fortune. It was a typical country farmhouse—old but comfortable with a warm, cozy feel that pleased her. She'd been lucky to get it for a price she could afford. She knew she owed it all to her real estate lady, Hailey Belle Sutton.

When they hadn't come up with anything that would work, Hailey had called her friend and the next thing Annie knew, this lovely place was offered to her. Hailey had told Lilly about Annie and Leo's situation—that they'd lost everything in a fire and they needed a furnished place, if at all possible. Though Lilly normally didn't rent her home out, she'd decided to do so for Annie and Leo.

She hadn't met her landlady yet but couldn't wait until Lilly came home from a trip out of town so she could thank her. Annie would never be able to tell Lilly how much her act of compassion meant to her.

The fact that the old homestead was surrounded by pastureland at the end of a dirt road for them to explore—as they were doing that morning—was even better. It reminded her of the ranch for abandoned and neglected girls she and Jennifer had lived in for a short time. Of all the foster homes they'd lived in, the ranch had been the best.

"Look, Annie Aunt, a baby calf!" Leo exclaimed after

they'd walked about half a mile into the back part of the property. They'd seen lots of cattle in the adjoining pasture, but this calf was right in front of them and on their side of the barbed wire. Before Annie could stop Leo, he bolted toward the small, fairly new calf.

"Leo, stop," she called, hurrying after him, her gaze locked on the momma cow that stood the distance of a football field away from the calf. Leo skidded to a halt when she hollered. He was only twenty feet from the calf. Startled, it began to wail as it bolted away from Leo.

At the baby's bawl, the momma's head whipped up and her big eyes flashed fire— *Oh no! This was not good.* Annie charged the same time the cow did.

"Run, Leo, run!" she screamed.

Leo's eyes grew wide and he couldn't move as he seemed transfixed to the spot, watching the huge cow barreling toward him. Annie reached him and scooped him up into her arms, her feet never slowing as she kept running. He screamed for her to hurry, as if finally finding his voice. The only thing remotely resembling a shelter was a scraggly tree not much bigger around than a flagpole. But at least it was better than a stalk of goat weed!

The mad bawling of the momma and the thunder of her hooves getting closer had Annie's feet moving as fast as they'd ever moved in her life. Breathing hard, she screamed for Leo to hold on when he started to slip from her grasp. He was so much heavier than she'd realized. Annie prayed for a miracle. Where she expected help to come from, she had no idea since they were alone in the middle of nowhere.

Breathing hard, she made it to the tree. Letting Leo

slip to the ground behind the tree, she turned to face the oncoming freight train.

Poor Leo was screaming and she realized she was, too. Holding her hand on Leo's shoulder, she prepared to play ring-around-the-rosies with the cow all day if that was what it took to keep him safe.

Momma cow charged the tree, and they scurried to the other side as it slammed its head into the thin trunk. It shook with the impact and Annie screamed again.

Dear Lord, *what* had she gotten them into?

Colt winced while struggling to rip open the bag of deer corn. Here in the deep woods the early morning quiet filled every space, and the sound of the bag ripping sent shock waves crackling through the stillness. The rustling of leaves told him he'd scared half the wild kingdom in the process of getting the bag open with one hand.

Watching the deer come into the clearing behind his cabin every morning and evening gave him some small semblance of… He couldn't call it peace—it was more a calming of the dark emotions lurking inside him these days.

Watching the deer come in droves to the corn was a positive sign. And with the drought that Texas had suffered through the last few months, the poor animals were hungry. Their ribs were showing worse than any time he'd ever known. They were so grateful for the corn.

Picking up the coffee can he used as a scoop, he dug it into the hard yellow corn, then began sprinkling the food along the ground, softened by the many hoofprints from the previous night's feeding.

As he'd done too many times to count, his thoughts drifted to the woman and the little boy. He'd hated the way he couldn't deal with Leo hanging on him and looking up at him with those adoring eyes.

Colt didn't deserve those emotions shining up at him from Leo's heart.

The aunt had been angry with him. He had seen fire flash a couple of times when she thought he wasn't doing right by Leo. He'd not been able to shake the feeling that he'd missed something. But then, he wasn't firing on all cylinders lately.

Digging the coffee can into the corn again, he sprinkled it out in a wide pattern and repeated the action several times. He needed the solitude that was here in his woods, needed to be away from people—being around Leo and Annie had solidified that belief. And yet, he was restless. And he figured he always would be. All the people who'd offered him advice had said that time would heal. He knew it wouldn't. He couldn't imagine time taking the slightest edge off the guilt he felt. Because no matter what his brothers tried to tell him, he knew in his heart that he could have stopped that wreck if he hadn't been so tired. He'd known his mind was fuzzy and his head had bobbed several times. Try as he might, he couldn't remember the impact of the wreck. He couldn't remember that moment when he had seen what was happening. He couldn't remember whether his head had been down and he'd been asleep when that drunk had hit him.

Had he been asleep at the wheel when that car had come across the yellow line and hit him, sending him plowing into the oncoming traffic? It was a question he would forever ask himself. And yet, what did it matter? He knew how much like soggy bread his thoughts had been and how elastic that had made his response time.

He knew.

And there was no amount of time that would distance him from that knowledge.

Nope, he was responsible for killing that family and he would have to live with that for the rest of his life.

There was no prison sentence harsh enough for what he'd done, so a life sentence of guilt was a most just penalty.

Having a child look at him with hero worship in his eyes had almost killed him.

He hadn't been able to take it—and so he'd run.

Here in the solitude of his woods, for now, was where he belonged. At least until he figured out how to deal with this.

His fist tightening around the cup, he jammed it deep into the corn, then slung the hard yellow kernels in a violent arch. Almost in the same instant, shouts echoed in the distance.

Screams.

Colt froze, thinking at first he'd flashed back to the night of the wreck. When the screams came again, shrieks of unmistakable fear, he knew better.

Colt bolted into action. Tossing the coffee can to the ground, he ignored the pain shooting through his collarbone as he charged through the woods in the direction of the screams.

It was coming from the old Tipps place. But Lilly kept that property empty. Or had up till now.

The yells were getting closer. He raced, pushing

through scraggly limbs, dodging rocks and fallen logs. Two people by the sound, one of them a woman and one a child. It was about two hundred yards between his cabin and the fence line that separated the two properties. Heart pounding with adrenaline and worry about what he would find when he got there, Colt did not let up as he ran. Briars tore at his arms and face, as he could use only one hand to brush them out of the way. His broken collarbone screamed at him in pain with each stride. He ignored it and focused on the two ahead of him.

He reached the fence quickly despite it seeming as though he'd been moving in slow motion. He could see them before he reached the fence. Annie Ridgeway and Leo standing behind a pitiful excuse of a tree as a blistering-hot momma cow charged them. Colt planted his good hand on the top of the wooden post, and catapulted himself over the fence. Grimacing, the pain very nearly brought him to his knees when he landed.

No time to waste, he began yelling to draw the cow's attention his way. "Yah!" he yelled, loud and gruff. "Get on outta here."

Annie and Leo whooped excitedly when they saw him charging across the pasture. The momma cow halted in its tracks, looked at him and then started to charge them again.

"Yah, yah!" Colt yelled louder. Coming up on the left side of the ol' gal, he saw her calf in the distance. So that was the problem. They'd gotten between her and her baby and she wasn't happy.

He waved his good arm, charged at the cow for a few steps, making her think he was coming after her, and she decided to take the baby and run. Tail tucked, she trotted away, glaring back at him once as if to dare him to come after her baby.

"Colt, Colt!" Leo exclaimed, racing from behind the sapling.

Seeing two Leos running toward him, Colt fought off dizziness and willed the pain that shuddered through his shoulder to go away.

"Boy, it sure is good to see you," Leo said, sliding to a halt in front of him. "I thought we was done for! Yessir, I sure did."

Annie was breathing hard when she reached him. Fear shone in her eyes like red flags, intertwined with relief. "I don't know where you came from, but—" Her voice broke and she visibly fought down the need to cry. "I'm so glad you came."

"That was one mad momma." Leo's voice squeaked from having screamed so much.

"Yeah, it was." Colt patted the kid on the head, pulling his gaze from Annie. "You've got to always go cautiously when you're around mommas and their babies."

"We were just walking, checking out the place, when Leo spotted the calf and raced off toward it. He didn't see the momma," Annie explained, her breathing finally getting back to normal. "I almost didn't get Leo away from her. If you hadn't shown up…" Her lip trembled and her unspoken words hung between them.

"You would have figured something out," he encouraged her. Something told him she would have, too. His own fear subsided a little bit as they stared at each other.

"So where did you come from?" she asked, pressing a hand hard against her stomach as if holding back her fear.

He yanked a thumb back over his shoulder to indicate the direction he'd run from. "My place backs up to this one. My cabin is just over that fence and through the woods a little."

Annie's jaw dropped. "You've got to be kidding."

"He don't have to be kidding, Annie Aunt! I like it," Leo exclaimed.

Colt chuckled. "I'm just as surprised to find you here as you are to find me here. Lilly doesn't usually rent this house out."

"That's what I was told. It's perfect for us, though."

"We didn't even know you lived in the woods." Leo laughed, the joy in his eyes dug into Colt like pins and needles. "Ain't that just a big ol' kick in the pants?"

"Leo," Annie warned.

"Sorry," he said, looking up at Colt as if he were about to get thirty lashes. "I'm not supposed to say 'kick in the pants.'"

"You are also not supposed to say 'ain't,'" Annie added, tugging gently on his ear.

He sighed. "Or 'can't,' either."

She chuckled at that, sending a warm shot of sunshine through Colt. It spread over him like rays melting ice, while she studied him with her pale gray eyes that again looked almost lavender in the morning light. Looking at her, it hit him how pretty she was. It wasn't something he'd noticed earlier, and it startled him to be noticing now. She had a simple, quiet look about her, a peacefulness. It drew him to her and he couldn't take his eyes off her.

Colt was startled by the attraction. It felt nice, and so did smiling and chuckling as he'd been doing since he'd hopped the fence. But it also felt wrong.

Feeling the sunshine she'd sparked inside of him fading into the darkness, he fought to hang on to it. All the while knowing he didn't deserve to feel that warmth and goodwill.

His gaze lingered on her. She was thin, but today her jeans and blouse fit her better and she didn't look as rail thin as he'd thought. Yesterday he'd believed she looked as though she was wearing someone else's ill-fitting clothes. Today, knowing about the loss of her home, he realized she very well could be wearing clothes she'd received from others after losing her things in the fire.

"Can I come over to see your house sometime?" Leo asked, tugging on his shirtsleeve.

"Come over. To my house?" Colt repeated the question, totally caught off guard.

"Yeah, your house. Can I come?"

He didn't want Leo coming to his house. But looking down at the kid's big smile, despite not wanting to feel anything, Colt felt stinging prickles of warmth. Like water on frostbite, feeling crept through him. "No—" The harsh sound of his own voice stopped Colt midsentence. He'd already run from the kid yesterday and he wasn't proud of it. Seeing the light dim in Leo's eyes cut straight into Colt's icy-cold heart.

Suddenly Colt knew he couldn't kill that light, no matter how unworthy he felt of such adoration, could he?

Chapter Four

"Leo, it's not nice to invite yourself to someone's home," Annie said, trying to distract Leo's attention. The child was persistent—which was nothing new to her. She'd known him for six years and he'd been persistent from the beginning, when he'd come into the world a month early after several weeks of trying over and over again to arrive early.

Though she shouldn't be surprised at the harshness of Colt's words, she was.

Call her crazy, when she saw the man come vaulting over the barbed-wire fence to their rescue, Annie had almost heard trumpets announcing that the cavalry had arrived!

Looking at Colt now, she couldn't think straight. Mere seconds ago she was so happy to see him that she very well might have run to him and flung her arms around his neck. Even kissed him, she was so out of her mind with relief. Now, he was lucky she didn't haul off and kick him in the knees.

"No." Colt placed his hand on her arm. "He can come. I'm sorry. It's, well, it's complicated."

"You mean it! I can come to your house?" Leo exclaimed, giving Annie a moment to gather her wits about her.

On the one hand, the fact that Colt was apologizing was a good thing. On the other hand, the man had his hand on her arm and electrical jolts were pulsing through her arm straight to the pit of her stomach. His gaze was locked on hers, too, with an intensity that could have knocked her over if she had been any shakier.

"Sure you can," he told Leo.

"Complicated" Colt had said—the cowboy had no idea *how* complicated it was, and it was getting more so with every passing moment.

For Leo, and for the fact that the man had just saved them, Annie relaxed and gave him a free pass.

"That would be a thrill for him," she said, pulling her arm away.

Hastily he drew his hand back as if he hadn't realized he'd been touching her. She couldn't get over the fact that he lived practically in their backyard. How in the world had that happened? Still, of all the places for her to rent… This was not divine intervention, was it?

She was standing in a pasture with Leo and his father, and that was either an odd coincidence or a God thing, only time would tell.

Colt stared at Leo, a curious expression on his face. The two of them were locked in conversation about where exactly Colt's cabin was. Leo had his hand hiked to his hip and his left leg slightly bent. He'd stood like that when he was in conversation ever since he was old enough to do so. He cocked his head to the side slightly and dipped his chin.

Colt was standing exactly the same way.

Annie's heart started hammering. Colt's eyes shifted to her, holding her gaze before he moved his attention back to Leo with the same contemplation. Annie's hand went to where the collar of her blouse would be, but she forgot she was wearing a collarless shirt! Instead she ran a finger along the edge of her neckline in a nervous movement that in no way matched the clanging alarm in her head. Colt was taking it in—seeing the uncanny mannerism of Leo. The one that she had seen all his life, never knowing till now he'd acquired it from the genes of his father. Genes that ran deep despite the boy having never been around Colt in person.

Suddenly Annie saw other things she'd never seen before. Things that a photo hadn't picked up on. Such as the way Colt's eyes flashed sharply with intelligence. It was the same way Leo's flashed when he was learning new things.

"Well, thanks for coming to our rescue," she blurted out, anxious for Colt to leave. She didn't want him figuring things out before she'd decided what she really wanted to do.

"Have we ever met before?" Colt asked, not taking her hint.

His eyes flashed with curiosity. Annie could practically see him rifling through his memory trying to place why she and Leo looked familiar. She knew she and Jennifer looked enough alike that people could tell they were sisters. However, there had never been a huge, jump-right-out-at-you resemblance. There was a similar thing that had gone on between them that was going on between Colt and Leo. Annie and Jennifer had the same expressions in different faces. They had the same voice and when she laughed there was a similarity. Not that Annie had had anything to laugh about since they'd come here, but she suddenly wondered how close Colt and Jennifer had been. Would he recognize Jennifer's laugh if Annie forgot herself and really got tickled about something?

"No. I don't think we've met." She forced the words.

He grimaced, favoring his collarbone for a moment.

"You are hurting." Annie changed the subject. "I know all that running and vaulting over the fence could not have been good for your injury."

"I'll live." He gritted the words out as he pressed his bent elbow closer into his side, adjusting the strap of his sling.

"And so will we, thanks to you." Gratefulness filled her up to overflowing.

"You both just seem so familiar to me," he said, stuck on figuring out who they were—maybe distracting himself from the pain that she imagined was stabbing through his broken bones.

"I ain't never met you in person," Leo said, bless his little heart. "I been want'n' to meet you, though."

Colt almost smiled. "Right. Maybe you both just remind me of someone. Anyway, I'm glad y'all are safe and that I heard y'all's yells for help."

Annie wanted to groan with relief as Colt changed the subject.

Leo edged closer to Colt. "I won't ever forget you jumping over that fence. You looked like you could fly." He held his arms out and pretended to fly. Colt laughed, shocking Annie.

He seemed as shocked by his laughter as she was. One minute it was rumbling out of him and the next he clamped his lips together and cleared his throat. It was as if he was rusty at laughing. As if he didn't want to laugh.

"Look, I better walk y'all back to your house and then I'll call Cort and tell him what happened. We'll make sure that momma and calf are put into another pasture farther away from the house. You should be able to take a walk without worrying about getting trampled. If y'all are going to live here, Leo needs to be safe."

"Aw, I can learn to scare them cows just like you did." Leo grinned up at his hero. Though they didn't look alike, there were indisputable similarities in Leo's expression and that of Colt.

Her nerves shook like brittle autumn leaves clinging to a branch. Colt shifted his gaze from Leo to her, then back to Leo once more.

He's seeing more resemblances with each passing moment. Right along with me.

Annie braced herself for his questions to resume.

"You're sure we haven't met? There's something about Leo that seems so familiar. Of course, I've met a bunch of kids at the rodeos."

The clock was ticking. She wasn't sure how long it would be before Colt realized that the child reminded him of himself. For that matter, she wondered who else would spot the resemblance. There was nothing for her to do about it right now except pray that God left blinders on everyone long enough for her to figure out what her next move was going to be. All she could do right now was act as though she had nothing to hide.

What better way to find out what kind of man Colt really was to live nearby?

So far her arrival in Mule Hollow had been nothing like she'd expected. Then again, when Colt found out why she was really here and what secrets she was keeping, how would he react?

How would the kind folks of Mule Hollow act?

Annie understood why the clinic needed help. Staring at the books the next morning, she was floored by how busy the small clinic was. Being the only clinic within at least sixty miles, Susan Turner had plenty of clients. Especially taking into consideration that Mule Hollow was surrounded by ranches, many of them fairly large operations. There was no end to the varying array of procedures she was hired to do. That, plus small animal checkups, left her and Gabi very little time to keep up with the paperwork.

Paperwork was Annie's specialty.

"So what do you think?" Susan asked after they'd gone over the books and the scheduling. "Do you think you can help us out?"

"I can," Annie said confidently. Susan was a willowy blonde who looked more like a model than a vet. She had long blond hair pulled back into a thick, lush ponytail that looked more glamorous than practical. It was obvious, though she didn't look the part, she was an excellent vet.

Gabi, on the other hand, was fresh faced, dark haired and had an athleticism to her movements that fit in with her career choice. Her energetic zest was evident, and there was no doubt in Annie's mind that she was the best at what she did.

"It's obvious the two of you have a great system. I'm not bragging, but I can promise you that I can handle this and even help streamline some procedures in the bookkeeping and paperwork department."

Susan smiled broadly. "I'll forever be in your debt if you can do that!"

Annie liked both women on the spot. Listening and observing how the two women spoke and treated each other, Annie noted that there was mutual respect and friendship here. She hoped that maybe she'd be able to be included in that over time. Even now, on her first morning, she felt the warmth of true welcome and, given the chance, she knew she could be a benefit to this business.

She said a quick thank-you to God for supplying this job to her. In the midst of the stressful situation she was here to address, having a job she was at peace with and enjoyed was going to be a real blessing. She ignored the pang of guilt that thudded like an undercurrent beneath every breath she took.

"So, now that we have that all settled…" Susan leaned against the counter. Holding a bottle of water between her hands, she toyed with the cap. "Gabi tells me you and Leo are big fans of Colt's."

"Leo is." The undercurrent turned into a riptide, the easy feeling of seconds ago swept out to sea. "I mean, you know, Leo loves bull riding."

Gabi poured herself a cup of coffee from the sideboard. "If you aren't a fan, then who taught him to be?"

Annie knew she couldn't keep Jennifer hidden for long. Everyone knew Leo was her nephew, so obviously there had been a sibling. "My sister, Leo's mom. She was the rodeo fan. She passed away last year." Gabi and Susan both gave their condolences. "Thank you. Jennifer never found a rodeo she didn't like." She didn't add that she also had never seemed to find a cowboy she didn't like. To this day Annie couldn't understand her sister's behavior.

"So you've raised Leo since last year?" Susan asked.

"Actually, I've been helping raise him since the day he was born. My sister moved in with me so I could help with him. He's like my own son, really."

"I'm so sorry he lost his mother. Thank goodness he's had you."

"I know this sounds nosy," Gabi said. "What about his daddy? Is he in the picture?"

Annie felt as if sharp gears were grinding to a halt inside her chest. It wasn't as if she hadn't expected that question. She'd answered it many times before. But being here, so close to Colt, made things different. "He's never been in the picture."

Susan's and Gabi's gazes met as the tension in the room spiked. Annie looked away quickly, trying to tell herself once again that she was being paranoid. Gabi had only met Leo briefly the day before. Imagining that she'd put the pieces of the puzzle together when she didn't even know there was one was just plain crazy.

She was going to have to have to get a handle on her mind. And she was going to have to do it soon.

Colt had racked his brain, ever since finding Annie and Leo next door to him, trying to figure out who Annie reminded him of. Both of them, actually, because there was something more familiar about Leo than Annie. But try as he might, it wasn't coming to him. Not that his memory was what it used to be. Since the wreck, there were holes in his memories.

Restless and wishing he had the use of his arm, he found himself toying with the idea of going to see if his new neighbors were home. The thought hit him like a kick in the chest from a bucking bronc. Truth was he'd taken about all the sitting around he could take. But he wasn't going to see Annie. He'd acknowledged that he was attracted to her, and was startled by the fact, since his heart felt as cold and hard as steel. The last thing he wanted was to tempt himself to seek out any kind of pleasure. It wasn't right.

But she kept easing into his thoughts without his realizing it.

Needing something to occupy his mind with other than thoughts of the wreck and his new neighbors, he headed toward the ranch office. He was about to get into his truck when he heard someone call his name.

Leo.

The little kid, dressed in blue jeans, T-shirt and boots, came tromping from the trees, the rope Colt had given him clutched tightly in his hand. When he saw Colt, his eyes lit up and he started running.

"Colt!"

Annie was nowhere in sight as Leo skidded to a halt in front of him. "Hi, Colt. I came to see you," he declared, as if he hadn't just walked across a pasture and through a small stand of woods.

"Yeah, I see that. You look like you came to learn to rope."

"I did. I brung my rope and ever'thing."

Colt glanced back at the woods. No Annie. "Is your aunt coming?"

Leo kicked a rock with the toe of his small boot, and his shoulders drooped slightly. "She was busy."

"Busy?" And she'd let the kid walk all the way across the pasture by himself, and then wander through the trees looking for Colt's cabin? He hadn't known Annie long but he knew this didn't sound right. Colt stooped to eye level with Leo. "Little buddy, does your aunt know you're here?"

Leo shrugged, not quite looking him in the eye. "She knows I went outside to play."

The poor woman was going to be frantic when she realized Leo was gone. It took a while to walk the distance between houses, so he was pretty certain she was already searching for him.

"Come on, we better get you back home."

"Aw, do we have to? I wanted to come see you."

"And I'm glad you did. But from now on, you're going to need to let your aunt know what you're doing, because she'll worry about you. Matter of fact, it's probably not a good idea for you to come all this way by yourself."

"You think Annie Aunt's gonna be mad?"

Colt grinned at the kid before he could stop himself and he tousled Leo's blond hair. "Maybe. But, come on… I'll face her with you. When a man messes up, he has to face the music."

Leo looked at him strangely. "I don't think she's gonna sing to me."

Colt laughed. "Probably not. But we've still got to go face her."

* * *

"Leo!" Annie scanned the pasture while she jogged, hoping to see him. But he was nowhere. She'd been unpacking some of their things in the bedrooms while Leo played with his rope in the backyard. When she'd checked on him twenty minutes later, he was gone.

"Leo!" she called again. Stopping to catch her breath, she scanned the pasture. He hadn't been in the barn or the front yard. He hadn't answered when she'd called his name over and over again. And then she'd thought about Colt. Leo had asked her on the way home from day care if he could go to Colt's, and she'd told him that today wasn't a good day.

Please let him be okay. Please.

She started moving again, just topping the slight hill when she spotted them. Colt and Leo walking side by side, crossing the pasture. *They walk alike.* The thought registered in the back of her mind, but she was too overwhelmed with relief for the implications to completely register. Gasping, Annie rushed forward.

"Leo! Honey, you scared me," she scolded, though she was so relieved it was a wonder she could speak. Scooping him into her arms, she hugged him tightly, fear washing over her. "Please don't go running off like that. Please."

"I'm sorry," he said, squirming as she set him back on the ground. "I just wanted to see Colt."

"I brought him back the minute I realized you weren't with him."

Colt's quiet words steadied her and she drew back from some of the terror that had clutched her. She tried to force the overreaction away. "Thank you. I feel awful.

I was unpacking and he was right outside roping. I didn't check on him for twenty minutes, so I didn't know how long he'd been gone. And then I had to check the barn and the area around the house." She was rambling and couldn't seem to stop it.

"He's fine. I don't think he'll be doing that again. Will you, buddy?"

Leo shook his head. "Colt told me I made you worry."

"I know you didn't mean to." She fought to let the episode go as she brushed his bangs off his forehead. "I'm just glad a cow didn't get you."

Colt's brows lifted a bit and he gave a slight nod of agreement.

"I was real careful. I crouched down real low, like this." Leo leaned over, hunkering down and demonstrating how he'd scurried across the pasture. When he came to a stray clump of bitterweeds, he crouched down, looked about, then grinned at them. "See, I was real careful and watched out for mean ole heifers like y'all told me to."

Colt and Annie laughed.

Then Leo headed home, continuing to sneak back across the pastures, obviously enjoying his game. Watching him, Annie and Colt began walking.

"Are you okay? You seemed...really upset."

Self-conscious, she sure wished she hadn't let her fear show. "I'm fine. I just got worried. Leo was gone."

He didn't say anything for a moment, just walked beside her, as they kept Leo in sight. "So, y'all are settled?" he asked, tucking his hands into his pockets.

Annie nodded, glad for a change of subject. "Pretty much. We really didn't have a lot to unpack."

"So, y'all lost everything?"

"Except each other." Annie met his questioning gaze. "The fire was bad. I'm grateful Leo wasn't harmed. If I'd lost him…or he'd lost me…" A lump lodged in her throat. "*That* would have been the tragedy." Her heart raced again at the thought.

Every time that horrible day came to mind, especially the moments when she'd believed she was going to die not knowing what had happened to Leo, she had to fight not to tear up. Forcing herself to the bright side, she smiled. "Thankfully, we have each other, and we're here in this neat little town, moved into this fantastic, quaint farmhouse that I've totally fallen in love with. I feel like I'm living on a smaller set of *The Waltons* when I'm in the kitchen."

Colt stopped walking. "So you were home when the fire happened?"

"I was. Leo was staying in town at a friend's house, because we knew our area was in a danger zone. When the fires struck it happened so quickly…" She paused, remembering. She rubbed her arms as Colt watched her with intense eyes. "It's unbelievable how your life can change in a flash," she added. Though she'd rather change the conversation, something in his expression, in his eyes, seemed to draw the words from her.

"Yes, it is." He took a deep breath and studied Leo, who'd reached the yard and had begun trying unsuccessfully to rope a bucket he'd set out.

Annie felt sad. Among all the other things she thought she'd seen in him at their first meeting, she'd glimpsed what she believed to be sadness. She'd chalked it up to the fact that his injury must have taken him out of contention for the national championship. Now she wasn't so sure.

"Have you eaten?" she asked impulsively. After all, she was here to find out who Colt Holden was. What better way to do that than to share a meal with him? "Leo would be ecstatically happy if you were to eat supper with him. I've got plenty."

"I haven't eaten, but—"

"Please join us. It's the least I can do after you've saved the day, two days in a row. I promise you it won't become a habit." As if she could promise that when Leo was around! What was she thinking? *You're thinking about making this man laugh again and you know it.*

He had a nice, rusty laugh and seemed to surprise himself every time one escaped the tightly guarded wall that surrounded him.

His eyebrows knitted slightly over deliberating eyes that darted back to Leo. Sensing their gazes, Leo looked up and waved. "Come help me, Colt." His little voice was full of excitement.

Annie held her breath.

"I need—" Colt started, and Annie was certain he was going to say, "I need to go." But he clenched his jaw and swallowed hard. If she'd hadn't already picked up that something was wrong in Colt's life, it was very clear now.

"Please," she urged, touching his arm. His tortured eyes were fathomless when he turned them to her.

What had happened to this man?

He blinked and the agony was replaced with that semiblank facial expression she'd seen before.

"I don't know what's bothering you," she blurted out. "But I'm thinking maybe some company would help. Please stay."

Chapter Five

Colt couldn't turn Annie's invitation down. Oh, he'd tried. She was persistent, though, and despite the loss and guilt raging through him, when she'd touched him, when he'd looked at her, he couldn't turn and run. Couldn't tear himself away even though he tried.

"Great!" A warm smile spread across her face and crinkled the edges of her eyes. Immediately she headed toward the house, probably afraid that he would change his mind. "Not that I'm promising anything fancy. But with Leo around, I can always promise wonderful, entertaining company."

She shot him a grin. "That kid'll brighten any day."

Colt took a deep breath. She had no idea that it was the little fella's exuberance and liveliness that had him twisted into knots right now. He pushed the idea away. He had to come to grips with this somehow. It would be just like God to move Annie and Leo right in beside him to help him to dig up out of the hole he was in. It didn't sit well with Colt, but that beef was between him and God; Annie and Leo had nothing to do with it.

* * *

Through the kitchen window, Annie watched Colt show Leo how to hold the rope and then toss it. Over and over it missed, and over and over Colt patiently showed him how to do it. Annie was supposed to be setting the table and putting the hamburger skillet dinner out, but she was drawn to the window to watch them. There was just no denying that Colt intrigued her.

The little voice in her head kept telling her he looked great, too—but she was ignoring the bothersome voice. Colt was crouched on Leo's level and was explaining how to hold his hand as he held the rope, and she was seeing yet again how similar Leo's movements were as he copied the way his daddy held his hand. So engrossed was Annie that it took a minute to realize she smelled something burning and that the room had somehow filled with smoke. "Oh, my goodness!" she exclaimed rushing over to the stove, where the skillet of hamburger and noodles smoldered!

"Nooo!" She snatched a potholder, grabbing the skillet handle—

"Annie Aunt, what'er you doin?"

Annie spun around, still holding the skillet with its smoking contents. "I…I'm—" Before she could say more, Colt crossed the room and turned off the flame of the gas stove.

"Maybe you should sit that back down now," he drawled.

Annie prayed that the earth would swallow her up, and rescue her from this major embarrassment. No such luck.

"That stinks," Leo said, scrunching his nose into a tiny contortion. "Are we gonna *eat* that?"

Colt, to his credit, didn't say anything. She knew what he was probably thinking—that he'd had to rescue her yet again after she'd told him he wouldn't have to. What in the world must the man think about her?

"I haven't gotten used to an electric gas stove yet," she said. And it was the truth. "The heat is either too high or too low."

"I understand that. I'm a gas stove man myself. Those electric ones that tell you how to do everything except dry and fold your laundry drive me crazy."

Annie chuckled, feeling less embarrassed. She hadn't been feeling like herself ever since she'd come to Mule Hollow. And the reason was standing in her kitchen right now.

"So, if you burnt dinner, what are we gonna eat?" Leo asked, looking at her as if all the world depended on this meal.

Annie gave an exaggerated groan. "Your appetite is growing faster than you are. Don't worry, sugar, you're going to eat."

Colt grinned at him. "Would you eat one of Colt Holden's famous omelets?"

"Sure!" Leo exclaimed. "I ain't gonna turn that down."

She was startled by Colt's offer and her heart tugged at the way he grinned at Leo. Maybe, this could all work out. A surge of joy ran through her. But then…did she even have the fixings that went into an omelet? Please, please let it be so.

"Better yet, would you help me make my world-famous omelet?"

Oh, that got a huge nod from Leo that Annie thought was going to break his little head right off his body.

"Do you have eggs?" Colt asked.

Heading to the fridge, Annie worried about how many she had as she tugged open the door and pulled out the container. She cringed. "I have only four."

Colt looked from her to Leo. "Well, how about this. I've got plenty of eggs at my place. What about y'all drive me to the fence line, we walk over to my cabin and then have dinner there?"

Annie felt the oddest tremor in her stomach. Who was this guy? He was definitely not the same guy they'd met yesterday morning.

"Can we, Annie Aunt? Please."

There was no way she could turn this down, and there was no reason to. She'd come here to get to know Colt Holden, and God had paved the way for that to happen.

Still, she would not be swayed after only two days. "We'll come over, but only if you're sure."

He hesitated for a brief moment and a shadow passed across his expression. "I'm sure."

Annie's insides quivered. All the way to his house, she told herself this attraction was understandable. The man was gorgeous and he was being kind to Leo.

Leo. She needed to remind herself that this was about Leo. Going to Colt's was a good chance for her to see Leo's daddy in his own home. What could be better than that? With the constant fear of someone realizing how alike Colt and Leo were, she was thankful that things were moving along so quickly.

Otherwise she didn't know what she was going to do.

* * *

"Now for my secret ingredients." Colt handed Leo a green container that had Tony Chachere's Seasoning written across it. Annie had seen the Creole seasoning but never used it. "This is a little spicy, but you're going to like it. Give those bad boys a good shaking of that." He indicated the bowl of eggs and milk. Leo turned his big eyes up at him and grinned.

"You betcha." Leo accepted the can of spices, then turned it upside down and shook it like there was no tomorrow.

Colt grimaced. "Okay, that should do it." When Leo continued shaking the can of stout Louisiana spice, Colt took it from Leo's hand, laughing. He hadn't quite expected such an enthusiastic response. He met Annie's twinkling gaze across the kitchen. She was sitting at the small breakfast bar that served as his dining room table in the small two-bedroom cabin. She'd offered to help, but there was only so much room in his bite-size kitchen. So instead she sat and watched.

He wasn't sure what he was doing. Why had he asked them here? What had gotten into him when he'd said he would stay for dinner in the first place? He hadn't expected how easily he'd jumped into the situation with his offer to cook omelets. Looking at Leo twisted his guts by reminding him of the little boy who'd lost his life because of Colt, but he couldn't ignore that Leo drew him. Something about the little boy could not be ignored. The fact that his heart seemed lighter in Leo's presence—and Annie's, too, for that matter—did make his guilt heavier. He was going to have to deal with that, because there was no way he could tell the kid no. No way he could shove the kid away as he'd done at their first meeting, when he'd handed him the rope and driven off.

Colt had never been one to hurt kids. He'd had enough hurt in his own childhood, as a boy who knew his parents didn't care about him. There was no way he could add pain to a kid's life. Being a champion bull rider, he'd always had kids hanging around him and considered it a privilege to give them a little of his time. If giving Leo some of that time cost him in the way of guilty feelings and stomach pains, then so be it. Colt was just going to have to take it like a man.

For now, he had omelets to cook. And there was no way he was going to let himself burn their dinner.

"Do we pour it in the skillet now?"

Leo's question got Colt back on track. "Yes, we do. We've got our ham and cheese and our other ingredients in there—"

"And our secret ingredient!" Leo added.

"You bet we got that in there. Now our skillet is warmed up and here we go."

Leo watched intently as Colt poured a portion of the mixture into the pan.

"You fellas look like you could have your own cooking show," Annie said.

So the lady speaks at last. She'd been quiet, watching him and Leo cook. It was almost as if she didn't want to interrupt the good time the two of them were having. But his attempts at drawing her into the conversation hadn't kept her talking. He glanced at her. "*Colt and Leo's Cowboy Cooking* sounds good to me."

"I like it," Leo said. And Annie agreed, a smile beaming across her face.

The omelets came out great, if he did say so himself. Of course, he pretty much lived on them. Though there was food in his freezer—casseroles his mother and all the good ladies of Mule Hollow had brought over after the accident—he hadn't had the desire to pull them out. He hadn't had much of an appetite, and omelets suited him just fine.

When the food was ready, he slid each omelet from the oven where they'd been warming while he and Leo finished cooking all three. Setting them on the bar, he took a stool across from Annie and Leo sat beside him.

"This is gonna be great," Leo gushed with glee.

"I hope y'all like them," Colt said. "If not, there's always Sam's diner."

"We're going to love these," Annie assured him.

Something in her voice drew him for a closer look, and he could have sworn that her eyes weren't twinkling from happiness but from the threat of tears.

She blinked hard and what he'd thought were tears disappeared.

When they finished eating, she insisted on clearing the dishes. He and Leo went outside and he pulled his old roping dummy from the side of the house. A steer head with a body made of a metal rod with small wooden calf legs hinged to it, he'd practiced his roping as a kid on Old T-Bone.

"I never knew you was a roper," Leo said as he was gathering up his rope for the tenth or fifteenth time. The kid was persistent and relentless. Both great traits for a man.

"I started out doing both. Then I began focusing on bull riding because it was my passion."

Annie came out onto the porch then, and sat on the steps watching them. She had her chin propped in her palm, her elbow resting on her knee. "So that explains it. I couldn't figure out the thing with the rope, either. I was just assuming that all cowboys learned to rope at an early age." She smiled. "You know, like it's a requirement or something."

"It is, in a way. Some are just better at it than others."

"I'm gonna be great. And the same goes for bull riding," Leo declared, tossing his rope for good measure. It hit a horn on the steer head, and he grinned as though he'd roped the thing. "I touched it!"

Annie laughed in delight. Her laughter tickled something deep in the center of Colt's chest.

"Way to go, cowboy," Colt said, excitement filling him. "Give it another go and see what happens."

Biting his tongue as he concentrated, Leo recoiled his rope, then got his hands set exactly as Colt had taught him. Colt thought it was pretty funny that he sometimes had a habit of biting on the tip of his tongue when he was concentrating. He had to warn Leo later on to be careful doing that. He'd learned that, when he was in the saddle, concentrating and holding his tongue between his teeth, if a horse made an unexpected movement the first thing he'd done was bite down hard. Doing that a few times had taught him to stop the tendency. Still, it was cute seeing how intently the little guy worked at his task.

When he let the loop fly, Colt was holding his breath. When it sailed over one of the horns and stayed, he let out a whoop at the same time Annie did. Leo, however, didn't make a sound. He just stood there with his mouth open, staring at the roping dummy.

"I did it," he said at last in total awe. "Would you look at that— *I did it!*" he finally hollered and spun toward Colt. He slung his arms around Colt's knees and jumped up and down. "I did it. I did it!"

"Yes sir, little cowboy, you sure did." He held out his hand and Leo gave him a high five.

Pride spread through Colt's chest. And he remembered the first time he'd hooked a horn. It had been Luke who'd given him a high five. His older brother had always been there for him. Thinking back, Colt had always given thanks for his two brothers. As long as Colt could remember, Luke had been the one he went to for anything. His dad was a drunk, and Colt had learned early on to stay out of his way. And his mother, well she'd never seemed to be around. And then when he was eight, she'd left. Colt pulled his thoughts away from the past and focused on the smiling Leo. Something about the kid reminded him of his childhood. Maybe it was just the fact that he had no mother or father and had only his aunt Annie to rely on. Their pasts were similar in that way.

When he glanced at Annie, there was a worried crease in her forehead as she watched him and Leo. She had a lot on her shoulders. She probably worried a lot about Leo, and the responsibility in raising him up all alone.

She stood abruptly, startling Colt. "Thanks for the evening," she said. "But we'd better get back home. It'll be dark soon."

"Aw, Annie Aunt, I was just getting started."

"Leo, it's time. Thank Colt for helping you."

Though his eyes were full of disappointment, he obeyed his aunt. "Yes, ma'am," he said with no enthusiasm. "Thanks a bunch, Colt. I had the best time in my entire life."

Colt chuckled, despite knowing something had put a burr under Annie's saddle that had her suddenly so ready to leave. He walked them through the woods, and it didn't go unnoticed that it was Leo who did most of the talking. As he waved goodbye and watched them drive away moments later, he was certain that there was something on Annie's mind.

What could it be?

What had caused her to leave so suddenly?

Chapter Six

"He's about the cutest thing I ever saw," Norma Sue said on Sunday after church.

Annie stood behind the church with a group of ladies after the services were over. They were watching Leo play with some of the other children, and he'd run over and told all of them about getting to eat supper with Colt. Then, he'd run back to play with his friends, leaving her to deal with the knowing looks and smiles. Every eye turned immediately on Annie. Problem was she didn't know if Norma Sue was talking about Leo or Colt.

"Yes, I think Leo is a pretty special little boy."

"I think so, too," Esther Mae said. "And he sure does look like Colt. Look at that, he's even copying the way Colt stands. Now, that's hero worship if I ever saw it."

"Isn't that something," Norma Sue said, watching the way he stood with one knee cocked and his hand on his hip.

Annie's breath caught at their words and her gaze met Gabi's, who was among the small group. Gabi had sharp eyes that took in everything. Annie had learned during the few days they'd worked together that she was very good at noticing details. Annie got the weirdest feeling that Gabi had observed these similarities already. Watching Leo, she knew without a doubt that her days keeping this secret were numbered. And though the matchmaking posse might think the similarities they were seeing were from hero worship, she knew that Gabi would realize that she was seeing genetic traits rather than copied mannerisms.

She'd left Colt's cabin the other day worried about the same thing. She was going to have to tell him, and she was going to have to do it soon.

"And y'all had dinner out there?" Norma Sue said, changing the subject from Leo. "That's just wonderful. You know, that boy's been through a lot. The fact that he's socializing at all is a fantastic thing."

"He's needed something since that terrible wreck," Adela said. "He suffered so much emotionally and maybe…" She turned her electrifyingly blue eyes to Annie and a gentle smile played across her features. Annie didn't think she'd ever met anyone like Miss Adela. Goodness just seemed to radiate from her. "God is going to use little Leo, and you too, to help draw our Colt from the dark mire of guilt and grief that he's struggling with."

Esther Mae and Norma Sue immediately agreed.

"You don't know, do you?" Gabi asked, realizing that Annie was clueless.

Annie shook her head. "No. I've figured out that something must have happened, during the time of the fires, when I didn't have time to watch television or anything. The last time we watched the bull riding on television, he was competing and actually won. What happened to him? I just assumed that he got stomped by a bull."

"You tell her, Gabi," Esther Mae said, shaking her red hair. She fanned herself vigorously with the brim of her floppy straw hat. The cluster of daisies hung on for dear life. "It's just too upsetting to me to talk about. Poor young man."

Everyone else agreed and Gabi took a deep breath. "He was competing night after night. Some weekends he was hitting three rodeos—sometimes in different states. He was worn out from driving so hard. But his hard riding was putting him back on top of the ratings. He really felt like this was his year to finally win the National Finals Rodeo in Vegas. He'd come so close year after year that he had really been pushing himself this year to win. He was coming home to rest up a week before competing in last month's second Mule Hollow Homecoming Rodeo. He was worn out. On the way home a drunk driver hit him and knocked him into the other lane. His truck hit a car with a young family of four. All of them were killed, including the drunk driver. Colt walked away with basically no injuries to speak of."

Annie felt ill. She couldn't believe it. What must he have gone through knowing he'd killed that family? The horror of it was too much to think about, much less live with. No wonder he seemed so lost at times. "I can't imagine how he must feel."

"We've all tried to tell him it wasn't his fault. But he believes if he hadn't been so tired he'd have been able to prevent the wreck."

It all made sense. The ladies quickly told her how he'd tried to hide his grief riding bulls, but had then been stomped by a bull and forced to come home to re-cuperate. He'd holed up at his cabin alone for almost three weeks now.

And then she and Leo had shown up.

Annie left church with a lot on her mind. Only God's timing could have brought them here when Colt needed his son most to help him overcome this horrible tragedy. Annie felt it in her soul that this was true.

Gabi and Montana were chatting in the kitchen when Colt knocked on the back door of Luke and Montana's house. He'd agreed to come to Sunday-night dinner after Montana had dropped by and invited him personally, in-sisting that he come. His new sister-in-law was a force to be reckoned with. That was why Montana was ranking so well in the women's barrel-racing standings. She was attacking her dream in the same way he'd been attack-ing his own. They'd hardly had any time to get to know each other, since both of them had been on the road hit-ting the rodeo circuits so hard. In town for only a short time, she wanted to cook dinner for Luke's family.

So here he was.

"Colt!" Montana exclaimed when she pushed open the screen door. "I am so glad you came." She pulled him into the kitchen and gave him a hug. "Luke will be so pleased. Look who's here," she said, turning to Gabi.

Gabi grinned. "You've made our evening by showing up." She hugged him, too. His brothers had both done well when it came to finding the women they wanted to share their lives with. He hadn't expected either of them to get married for a while, but Luke had fallen fast and hard when he'd met Montana. And Jess had done the same when he'd met Gabi. Their wedding was coming up in a few weeks and he was happy for Jess.

Colt's head had been full of dark thoughts since he'd had Leo and Annie over. He'd gone from feeling a sliver of hope to taking a plunge into the guilt of having felt something other than disdain for himself. He'd recognized that being alone in the darkness wasn't a good thing. Montana had shown up at the perfect time.

"The guys are in the living room talking about cows and lack of rain." Montana pulled Colt over to the kitchen breakfast bar and pushed him onto the stool. "You need to stay right here for a few minutes and visit with the women in your life."

He smiled at that. Smiles were coming easier these days and he knew that was good. He couldn't continue to live in the dark hole that he'd buried himself in for the first few weeks after the wreck.

"That's right." Gabi pushed a plate of chocolate-chip cookies his way. "Is there anything we can do for you?"

Both women were watching him with compassion. His gut wrenched. "I don't know what to say. I'm doing all right." That wasn't the truth, but he wasn't sure how to voice the things that were going on inside his head. He'd never been real good at opening up.

He picked up a cookie, not because he had an appetite; he just needed something to occupy his hands.

"Hey, little brother," Jess said, coming into the kitchen. Luke followed him. They made a beeline for the cookies.

"Glad you came." Luke held the cookie up. "They made these for you and we couldn't have any until you got here."

Montana put her arms around Luke's waist as he slipped an arm around her. "You should have seen your brothers." She grinned at Colt. "They were pretty pitiful, trying to sneak some when they thought we weren't looking."

Jess finished his cookie and grabbed another. Gabi laughed, and he grabbed her, tugging her close. "Gabi's too observant. I think she has eyes hiding under that ponytail at the back of her head."

"I do, and don't you forget it."

Colt felt a stab of envy at the happiness around him. He was glad his brothers had found Gabi and Montana. Growing up, they'd been three kids just trying to get by. He'd hidden his emotions in dreams of becoming a rodeo hero, and as a youth he'd put all his energy toward making that dream come true. The idea of building hearth and home with someone was not even a blip on his radar, and any woman he met had to understand that.

In that moment, he thought of Annie. Of her sitting in his kitchen Friday night. His thoughts had been stuck on her and Leo ever since.

"I hope you're going to reconsider and be in the wedding," Gabi said, drawing his attention. "It would mean so much to us."

Jess nodded, his blue eyes watchful. Colt knew they were all trying to gauge how he was doing. The room suddenly hummed with tension. "I'm not sure if—" The disappointment he glimpsed in Gabi's eyes, when she knew he was about to tell her he wouldn't, stopped him. "I'll be in the wedding."

Thankfully the room didn't erupt into cheers. He couldn't handle that kind of emotion right now and they knew it. Instead slow smiles spread across everyone's faces as they all told him how glad they were that he would be there.

The sun was setting on the horizon about two hours later when they'd all eaten perfectly cooked steaks and baked potatoes. While the girls talked wedding plans, the guys gravitated to the back porch to talk about the ranch and the drought that was threatening everything they'd worked so hard for.

Jess and Luke had opted to sell some of the herd a couple of weeks back in order to make the hay last longer. They were being forced to purchase hay at an elevated price because of the lack of local hay. Colt had no real enthusiasm for the discussion now. His focus had never been on the ranch that Luke had wanted to own so badly. He understood his brothers' need for a place to lay down roots—something they'd never known. His older brother had been driven to build something in order for his and Jess's children to have a legacy. It stemmed from Luke's role as the leader of the family, ever since he was a kid.

Colt felt no need to settle down. He'd always had a restless spirit and nothing had changed. He was here only because of circumstances that were out of his control. When his collarbone healed enough for him to climb back on a bull, he'd be gone again. After what he'd done, even if he wanted a family, he knew he didn't deserve one. This ranch would be a legacy for Luke's and Jess's families. Not his.

"Colt, we need to talk to you about something," Luke said after Colt saw him and Jess exchange one of their it's-time-to-get-to-the-point looks that he'd begun to see often when the three of them were together.

He'd been expecting it all night long. Ever since Gabi had asked him about Annie and Leo coming over to his house for dinner. She'd heard about it at church today. He hadn't said much, and though they'd all let the topic drop, something told him it hadn't been forgotten. Gabi had seemed a little nervous to him tonight, and he'd attributed it to thinking about her upcoming wedding. When she'd asked him about Annie and Leo, he'd noticed she'd almost shredded her napkin picking at it.

"Yeah." Jess joined in, scooting to the edge of his chair and leaning forward, his elbows resting on his knees. Both of his hands were wrapped around his coffee mug when he met Colt's curious eyes with his serious ones. Luke's eyes were thoughtful, too.

Colt stilled himself for the talk about the wreck not being his fault and how he needed to pull himself out of the muck he was feeling and start moving forward. He was prepared for them to tell him they were glad he was spending time with Annie and Leo. It had occurred to him when Gabi had brought up the subject that the group would naturally start believing that was what he needed. Having Annie and Leo over opened the door for that kind of thinking. They were wrong.

"We, ah, we've noticed something," Luke continued, his words uncertain.

Luke's hesitation grabbed Colt's attention. A glance at Jess told him he was just as reluctant to talk about whatever was bothering them. Colt crossed his arms and waited.

"We've noticed things about Leo that—well, frankly,

they remind us of you." Luke snapped his mouth shut, and tensed his jaw. Jess nodded agreement, his own jaw rigid as he watched Colt.

"Something about him reminds y'all of me?" He thought about that for a minute. "I've been thinking I knew them from somewhere, because something about them is familiar to me. But Annie said we've never met." He looked from Jess to Luke. They were really acting strange.

Reminds them of me. A picture of Leo holding his rope as Jess had showed him came into focus. Another picture of Leo, cocking his head to the side, jumped out at Colt. "Yeah, the kid copies me," he said. "He's been watching me since he was in diapers, I think. His mother must have been a real PBR fan to have plastered pictures of me all over the poor kid's room."

"Don't you think that's a little bit odd?" Jess asked.

Colt hiked a shoulder. He hadn't really given it much thought. There were certain people, women especially, who were infatuated with him and his bull riding competitors. Some women seemed to be on the road from rodeo to rodeo as much as the riders themselves. He had let women like that distract him earlier in his career. But the last couple of years he'd barely given them a glance, hadn't spent any time with them. He'd realized that to win the championship, he needed all his focus to be on the bull. Nothing else mattered. Until everything had come crashing down.

"Maybe his mother used to be one of those women that followed me around."

Luke leaned forward and Jess straightened. Both brothers looked as though he'd just told them something they'd been waiting to hear. He studied them, his eyes narrowing. "What are y'all thinking?" He suddenly didn't like the direction this conversation was taking.

Luke cleared his throat. "It's understandable that you don't see what we're seeing. Truth is, me and Jess saw something that first morning. Then Gabi said something. And you know how alert Gabi is to detail." It was true. Gabi had proved that when she'd headed up the search for what was killing their cattle a few weeks ago.

"Gabi came home the first day she met Leo and told me the kid reminded her of you. She didn't think much about it at the time, because she didn't know about Leo's mother plastering pictures of you all over his wall. When I told her, she didn't say anything except that it seemed a little odd."

Colt's memory was suddenly shuffling through years of files.

Luke leaned forward again and his somber brown eyes hit Colt in the gut. "Is there a possibility you could have a son?"

"What?" Colt asked, thinking he had heard wrong. But one look at both Luke's and Jess's expressions and he knew they were serious. Dead serious.

"You said they look familiar to you. Maybe it's because when you look at Leo you see some of what we're seeing," Jess said.

"And we don't know what Annie's sister looked like. Maybe they looked alike," Luke added. "Do you think that's a possibility?"

"Well…" He rubbed the back of his neck with the hand of his good arm and thought about his past. He'd eased his loneliness with whoever happened to catch his attention. None of the relationships had ever meant anything and he'd always been careful.... Well, truthfully, he knew there were times when that just wasn't true. "The truth is, maybe."

"That would mean Annie moved here for some reason but is hiding the truth," Luke said. "I've only met her once, but I didn't get the impression that she was a deceptive person."

"I need to go," Colt said brusquely, standing so quickly that his collarbone retaliated painfully.

He stepped from the porch.

"Colt, what are you going to do?" Jess said.

"Don't do anything rash. It's only a hunch, nothing concrete."

Luke's words halted him. "I need to think. That's all. Tell Montana and Gabi I'll talk to them later."

He didn't slow down again until he was at his truck.

Was it true? Could Leo really be his son? Sure, there could be other explanations, but there was something about Leo that even he recognized as more than hero worship. Leo was only six, after all. The way he bit his tongue when he concentrated. And then there was the way he stood. Colt wasn't one to jump to conclusions. But he was going to observe both Leo and Annie more closely. Because if Annie had something to hide, then he was going to figure it out.

What are you going to do if it's true?

As he pulled his truck to the side of the road, gravel shot out from beneath his tires, and if he'd been on pavement he'd have burned rubber. He wasn't daddy material.

He'd never been daddy material and nothing had changed.

His hands tightened on the steering wheel and his forearms strained with the pressure as his thoughts raced.

What am I going to do if it's true?

"Annie, can you help me for a minute?" Gabi called, poking her head around the door of the clinic.

"Sure." Annie pushed out of her chair and hurried to follow Gabi into the back room. Gabi was standing by the squeeze chute out by the small outside corral. She and Susan were about to leave for an on-site vaccination job of a herd, and Susan was double-checking her supplies on her truck before she headed out.

"Annie, we'll be at Ross Denton's for most of the day, but if you need us, use the radio and you'll get us."

"Okay, I'll do that." She walked over to where Gabi was holding a contraption that looked like a hole puncher. Gabi had acted all morning long as if she had something on her mind. She'd been quiet, and Annie thought Gabi might be preoccupied with her wedding plans, but worried that it wasn't the case.

"Can you check the number on this heifer with the records and make me a printout?" Gabi's watchful eyes met hers.

"Sure." Annie wasn't certain how to take the look. Making a mental note of the number, she headed back into the office. Within moments she'd pulled the info up and took the printout back to Gabi. Susan was heading out by that time, leaving Annie alone with Gabi.

"Thanks." Gabi took the page and studied the information on it.

Annie turned and started to head back to the office.

"Did your sister go to many rodeos?"

Annie stilled her nerves at the question. She hadn't missed how Gabi had watched Leo from day one. Did she know? Annie was having a hard time hiding the truth of Leo's identity, but that was for his safety until she knew the right decision to make. But Annie couldn't lie outright to Gabi. When asked a direct question, she had to answer truthfully. "Yes, actually she did. Jennifer loved the rodeo."

Gabi tapped the printout on her thigh. "She liked bull riding especially. And Colt best of all?"

"Yes." Their eyes held on that answer. Annie waited for Gabi to say more. For her to come out and ask if her sister had spent time with Colt. After a minute, Gabi nodded, then turned back to her work.

Annie didn't move. She tried to decide whether to smooth out what had just transpired or to slither back into the office like the snake she felt she was. Had Gabi been waiting for her to tell her something? To make a confession about what she suspected?

Nerves rattling, Annie went back to the office. She had a big decision to make.

Chapter Seven

A sound woke Annie and she sat up in bed. Footsteps outside on the porch. Annie glanced at the clock—it was two in the morning. Who would be on her front porch at two in the morning? It sounded like there were a couple of people. Swinging her feet to the floor, Annie tiptoed to her door and listened. From her room it was a straight shot down the hall to the back door. Because the door had a paned-glass window in it, she peeked around the corner to see if she could see anyone. But it was dark on the porch, and if she saw shadows she couldn't tell.

There was a faint bit of light coming into the hall from the night-light in the bathroom next to the kitchen. The light glinted off the back doorknob. It was just enough light for her to see the doorknob turn. Someone was trying to get into the house!

Annie had had a bad day—she'd spent the rest of the afternoon at work attempting to keep her mind on track and do her work, while trying not to panic about telling Colt about Leo. Then she'd picked Leo up from day care and he'd been running a fever. She'd spent the evening getting his fever down and taking care of him, which had effectively halted any thoughts she'd had of going to Colt's and confessing. And now, to top off an already horrible day, she had someone breaking into her house!

Trying not to let the person or persons on the other side of the door see her, she peered around the bedroom door again. Squinting, she struggled to see who stood on the other side of the glass, but there wasn't even a shadow. The thudding, which sounded as if the people were tiptoeing in heavy boots, had her straining to glimpse the trespassers. Her heart pounded with fear.

What should she do? She'd never had someone try to break into her house before. Her heart thundered in her chest and her hands shook as she grabbed a candleholder off the dresser. She needed to get to Leo's room. And then she needed to get to her cell phone—it was in the kitchen. But who would she call? Cell service was terrible in the Mule Hollow area, and the ground line hadn't been hooked up yet.

"Do *not* panic," she told herself. "When I am afraid I will trust in the Lord. When I am afraid I will trust in the Lord." She muttered the Bible verse under her breath in a chant several times. Then moved silently down the hall and slipped into Leo's room. He was asleep and she gently touched his forehead, which was cool to the touch. *Thank you, Lord.* She sent up the silent prayer and then moved to the window.

Peering into the darkness, she saw no one moving about this side of the house.

She checked to make certain the locks on the windows were securely fastened. Then she tried to decide what to do. It was times like these that she really hated being single. She didn't think about her situation often.

Didn't think about how she had set herself up for a life alone. She'd never met a man she trusted. Not enough to allow herself to get close to him, to think about maybe sharing a life together. But it sure would be nice to feel protected.

A noise from the kitchen area set her back on high alert—a scratching sound from the windows around the breakfast area. Tiptoeing into the hall, she flattened her back against the wall and looked toward the kitchen window.

Colt sat on his back porch and stared at the stars. The moon was barely a sliver tonight, leaving his surroundings shrouded in darkness and shadows. Kind of how he felt on the inside. Colt believed in God. He'd given his life to the Lord years ago, but somewhere along the way he'd gotten off track. Started thinking about becoming a champion, being driven by that desire to prove something about himself. He'd gone to some of the church services held by rodeo preachers like Chance Turner, who'd hung up his traveling boots and settled in at the Mule Hollow Church of Faith. But most of the time he'd been too busy getting from one rodeo to the next. Or layin' in late from…"spending time" with one of his adoring fans. Colt's gut tightened with guilt.

Had he fathered a child from one of his so-called fans? Had he brought a child into the world by his carelessness?

Distressed, he'd almost driven to Annie's on Sunday night right after talking with Luke and Jess, but he'd caught himself. It wouldn't do anyone any good for him to go accusing someone of something this important while he was so angry. And he'd been angry, all right.

Holding back had taken a lot of effort as he'd paced the fence line between their houses most of the day and racked his brain trying to pull up a face from his past about seven years ago. Someone who reminded him of Annie. Or Leo.

Blank as a chalkboard, his mind had come up empty. Had he been with that many women? By the world's standards, no. But by God's standards, even one was too many. If she was the wrong one.

Is Leo my child?

If it turned out that he was, what was he going to do about it?

Annie blinked. Her heavy eyelids lifted and she had to think a minute to realize where she was—sitting on the floor in Leo's room beside the window, her back against the wall. She'd gone to sleep sitting here at some point before dawn. After wandering silently through the house trying to catch whoever was out there, she'd finally sunk to the floor here and waited. She'd thought that if they looked in this window she'd catch them. The candlestick lay on the floor beside her. Rubbing her eyes, which felt like they'd had a sack of sand poured into them, she turned her head to look out the window—*huge* brown eyes rimmed by long, dark lashes blinked at her!

Annie screamed, scrambling on all fours away from the window. Her heart thundered and her stomach was still over there plastered to the wall where she'd been. She turned around when she reached Leo's bed and, sure enough, there looking in the window was the hairiest big-lipped donkey she'd ever seen.

It watched her, batted the eye that was practically flattened to the glass pane, then turned its head and smashed those poochy lips to the glass as if giving the window a big, juicy kiss.

A donkey. After the surprise passed, relief set in as Annie realized this was her early-morning vandal.

"Whoa!" Leo was bounding off the bed behind her. "A donkey!"

As if in answer, the brown donkey rolled its big lips and grinned, exposing a mouthful of pearly whites. Annie laughed, as much from relief as from hilarity. Leo raced to the window.

"Hi, donkey," he called, leaning over and putting his face level with the animal. "I gotta see him," he said. Spinning around, he grinned, then raced out of the room.

Annie hurried after him. She didn't know if this was a dangerous donkey that might kick or bite him. "Leo, wait," she called, catching a glimpse of herself in the hall mirror as she passed. She looked frightful, with her hair all mussed and red-rimmed, sleepless eyes. Leo was out the door by the time she reached it. She was chasing him around the corner of the house when she saw Colt walking across the pasture.

She blinked her gritty eyes and raked a hand through her ratty hair, which looked as if a flock of pigeons had roosted in it. Having no time to worry how ghastly she looked, she hurried around the corner to the side of the house that Leo's window faced. Relief washed over her when she saw the fat little donkey, sitting on its haunches and letting Leo pet it. Both animal and child looked overjoyed at the experience.

Annie skidded to a halt and let out a breath of relief.

"Look, she likes me." Leo laid his head against the donkey's neck and hugged the rotund little female.

Annie chuckled, and walked over to scratch her between the eyes. "Well, hi there, you little trespasser." Who had scared her to death last night. She felt silly now, realizing that it was hooves tramping across her back porch that she'd heard. Then again, the doorknob had twisted. Could a donkey do something like that?

"Colt!" Leo exclaimed, looking past her. Annie turned to find Colt striding around the end of the house. His expression was dark, his gaze locking with hers and stilling her heart, before he gave Leo a strained smile.

"Hey there, Leo, I see you've met Samantha."

"Samantha, is that her name?" Leo asked, laying his head back against the donkey's mane.

Samantha laid her head to the side as if to touch Leo's head, gave a loose-lipped grin, then snorted. Her tail flapped furiously against the ground.

Annie chuckled, despite knowing that something was on Colt's mind.

"Samantha is her name. She belongs to Lilly, your landlady. She thinks she owns this place and Cort's since they got married."

Annie had met Lilly briefly, on Saturday. She was an energetic woman around Annie's age with a head of dark, springy curls and a cheerful smile. Annie hadn't known she owned a fat, little donkey that loved kids and enjoyed scaring single mommas to death.

"Can I ride her?" Leo asked, eyeing her wide back with interest.

Colt nodded. "From what I know about her, she is very kid-friendly, so that is a possibility."

"Awesome!" Leo exclaimed. Samantha stood up, showing off her odd shape. She didn't have smooth sides like your normal burro—but instead she was so chubby that she actually had a couple of rolls running horizontally between her front legs and her hind legs.

"Come on, Samantha," Leo crooned cajolingly, as he'd done when talking to the puppies the day of their arrival. He raced around in a circle, then jogged off. Samantha trotted behind him.

Despite the dull ache in the pit of her stomach, Annie chuckled. "That is a country boy's version of 'Mary Had A Little Lamb.' She is the oddest little burro I've ever seen."

"Yeah, I think the way she looks has to do with her getting into some old paint when she was small. She's very mischievous, used to come inside the kitchen of Colt's house, where she was raised prior to moving here, and eat bread out of the bread box. I think they said teeth marks are on one of the drawers."

"Oh, my. How funny. And she must be able to turn doorknobs, too. I was wakened by a noise about two this morning and was scared to death." She was rambling but she suddenly couldn't help it. "I thought someone was trying to break into the house. I could see the doorknob turning and then I heard footsteps on the porch. I ended up spending a sleepless night on watch sitting beside the window in Leo's room. That donkey was looking at me through the window when I woke a few moments ago. I must have dozed off…" Her words trailed off.

Colt didn't say anything, the tension radiating between them. Annie had struggled for days with how to tell Colt. Sometime between last night and this morning she'd decided she had to tell him he was Leo's daddy. When she'd settled in against the wall, it hit her all over again that Leo needed someone in his life other than her. If something ever happened to her, she'd never want him to go into the system—not when he had Colt for a father.

She started to chatter on, putting off what she knew she needed to do but wishing to be better prepared—to at least have had a hot shower and a cup of coffee. But Colt beat her to it.

"Annie. Is there something about Leo you haven't told me?" His eyes held the wariness of a man who'd been lied to. Betrayed.

Annie's insides trembled with the terrible knowledge that he knew she had a secret. She hated knowing she was the one he didn't trust. Inhaling slowly, suddenly, aware that she hated seeing that distrust in his eyes. Instantly she became aware of her appearance. Not much sleep, red, itchy eyes, crazy hair and her sloppy T-shirt and shorts—not exactly a look that inspired the kind of self-confidence she needed to hold this important conversation.

She raked a hand through her hair, her fingers snagging in tangles. She took a deep breath.

"I need to know what you aren't telling me," Colt said.

Annie ran her tongue over her lips, which suddenly

felt as parched as the poor Texas pastures surrounding them. The drought had nothing on her.

Leo's squeals of laughter drifted around the corner of the house. A loud *eh-haw* and several snorts followed. "Do you remember a Jennifer Ridgeway?"

She could tell he was shuffling through his memory and she wondered how many women he had to sort through to find that name. That face. She knew there were lots of women like her sister, who followed those cowboys around just waiting for the chance to meet and spend time with them.

"She was my sister," she offered when he remained silent. "She loved a good rodeo, and bull riders were her favorite. She went to see you ride many times." She could tell by the way his brow crinkled over his right eye that he was struggling hard to place the name. "She had light brown hair, was smaller than me and had gigantic brown eyes. She and Leo looked similar. She and I didn't look that much alike. Kind of like you not looking like your brothers."

"I can't place her. Or that name."

Annie couldn't take much more. She needed to tell him and end this torture. "She went by R.W. sometimes. Why, I haven't a clue."

Colt's shoulders tightened in reflex to the initials. "I remember an R.W."

There was no fanfare. No aha exclamation. Just the quiet acknowledgment that they were now on the same page. Annie wanted to throw up. "Jennifer died last year. Right before she died, she told me. She made me promise to keep it a secret, but she thought someone should know the truth. You are Leo's daddy."

* * *

It was what he'd known, from the moment Luke and Jess had told him their suspicions. He'd tried to talk himself out of believing it, but he'd known.

He had a son.

He closed his eyes and let the truth sink in around him. There was an undeniable joy that sprang forth, unexpected. But it was there. He held his expression in check, as anger surged through him. "Why wasn't I told?" And yet he knew the answer. He couldn't remember many details about R.W. She, like all the other women he'd met on the road, was nothing but a blur. For that he felt a sudden and hard sense of shame. Especially in light of knowing he'd fathered a child he hadn't even known about.

There was no one to blame but himself, and yet looking at Annie he did just that—blamed her for keeping Leo from him. "You came here with this knowledge. You knew for a year. What is it with y'all? A man has the right to know."

Annie moistened her lips and her eyes looked pained. She was a mess, and although it was obvious that she hadn't slept all night, her beauty still stood out. He ignored that. Deception in a pretty package—he had no use for it. She'd known for a year.

"Jennifer made me promise. I felt guilty once I knew, but I'd made the promise. And I had Leo's best interests to look out for. Leo is the bottom line here. What's best for Leo. Jennifer knew you didn't want kids. She knew your life was all about the rodeo and she accepted that. She also knew she didn't really know you as a man. That you and she were just two people…" She hesitated, as if searching for the words.

Her words were cutting to the core of him. Leo's well-being was what mattered. It was all that mattered.

She cleared her throat. "Jennifer knew she meant nothing to you. She chose not to tell you because she believed you didn't want to hear it. I wasn't sure what was right."

They stared at each other for a long moment. Colt's emotions were crashing against each other. "I need to go. I need to think." Turning, he started back toward the pasture. The long walk here had seemed a good idea when the sun came up, but now he just wanted to be away, and the last place he wanted to go at that moment was across the backyard and Leo's path…his child.

He had a child. And he wasn't sure what in the world to do about it.

Annie watched Colt stride off. She was speechless. What could she say? He'd looked angry—tortured and *angry*. She'd expected it. So why was she baffled by his attitude? Why indeed, when she didn't have a clue how to handle the next step in all this? How did she go about telling Leo that his hero was also his daddy?

She followed Colt at a distance. This would give them both a chance to regroup. She'd get her shower, a pot of hot black coffee and some much-needed time to think while she was at work. They could move forward later.

She found Leo trying to rope the docile Samantha, who stood still as a stuffed animal, not moving anything but her jaw as she munched on a long piece of grass.

Colt stood for a minute watching them. His good arm tucked in his jeans pocket.

"You're doing good, Leo," he said, his eyes cutting to her for a moment. "I'll talk to you later." The subtle displeasure was clear to Annie. She said nothing as she watched him head back across the pasture.

Annie's stomach growled, echoing the frustration she was feeling.

"Come on in, Leo, I need to check your temperature. Then it's time to get ready for day care if you feel better."

"Aw, Annie Aunt, I wanna stay home and play with Samantha. She's great!"

Despite everything, Annie laughed. Maybe it was just nerves, but suddenly she loved that little donkey for the distraction that she was and the friend she suddenly felt that she was going to be to Leo. "Maybe she'll hang around till you come home this afternoon. If not, then maybe Miss Lilly and Mr. Cort will let you go visit."

He beamed, walked over and threw his arms around Samantha's neck. "That'd be the best thing ever."

Annie's eyes filled with unexpected tears. Sweet boy. What was he going to do when he found out about his daddy?

A peace came over her and she knew telling him was going to be the easy part. The good part.

It was she and Colt who were going to have the problem. As it stood, neither one of them trusted the other. But she knew that when Colt realized she'd been trying to do the right thing for all involved, and that she had been trying to do what was best for Leo, he would understand.

Whatever happened between her and Colt was no

longer the issue. He was going to be a great asset to Leo's life. Leo was going to love having his bull-riding hero as his daddy. Leo was going to think *that* was the best thing ever!

Chapter Eight

As if it were meant to be, the books were not as filled up that day at work as they normally were. Susan was scheduled to be in the office for most of the day, and Gabi, too. After a very hot shower and a mental pep talk over two quick cups of very dark coffee, Annie had dropped Leo off at day care and raced to work. Gabi didn't have much to say to her. Though she wasn't ugly, she was definitely quiet. Since she'd been very friendly and helpful when they'd first met, Annie could no longer deny that Gabi knew, or heavily suspected, that Leo was Colt's child. Maybe she was unsure why Annie was hiding the truth or how to handle the situation. Annie agreed with her.

She usually liked to handle things in a straightforward way. But this way was odd, awkward and totally uncomfortable. Around midmorning it was Susan who took the bull by the horns.

"Okay." Susan propped her hip against the counter, as was her habit when she was in the office area talking or waiting on printouts of information and such. "I'm just going to hit this thing head-on. What's going on between the two of you? The tension in this room is as thick as Norma Sue's chocolate pie."

Knowing it was time to set things straight with Colt before talking to anyone else, Annie said, "If you don't mind, I need to take off for a few hours. Maybe the rest of the day. I really don't know for certain. I need to take care of something."

Susan looked from her to Gabi, crossed her arms and nodded. "Fine. When you get back, will this thing between the two of you be better?"

Gabi met Annie's gaze but remained silent. Annie swallowed the lump in her throat so she could continue. She really liked Gabi and didn't want this hanging between them. "I think so." It was all going to come out; however, until she spoke with Colt again, she wasn't saying anything to anyone. But she knew she had to do this. God had been leading her to this point all along. And though she'd been stubborn about much of the plan, she was on board now.

Susan headed toward the doors to the back. At the door she paused. "Take the day if you need it. And if you need to talk—either one of you—I'm here."

They watched Susan go and then Annie turned to Gabi. "Can you tell me how to get to Colt's cabin from here?"

Colt was standing on the front porch when Annie's old car came driving through the trees. A host of emotions had rolled through him since learning that Leo might be his: disbelief, joy, anger. He was glad he'd walked away this morning after confronting Annie.

Confronting Annie when Leo was around the corner

hadn't been a good idea. Plus, he'd needed to think, and Annie had said something that had pulled him back from the brink of making a major mistake. He'd been ready to demand custody of his son. Demand his rights and take back what was his. But Annie had reminded him that she'd been doing what she believed was right for Leo.

What *was* right for Leo?

That question plagued him. What was right for his son?

In the midst of his anger he'd lost sight of a lot of things. Calmer now, he knew Leo deserved better than him.

"I thought we needed to talk," she said, closing her car door and walking his way.

She looked like a reed in her jeans and white T-shirt, and he wondered if part of her thinness had to do with worrying about coming to Mule Hollow and meeting him.

"That'd be an understatement." He wasn't feeling any generosity toward her.

"I know you're angry, Colt. I'm sorry, and I can't do anything to help that now. But I'm here to work something out now. I'm here to set this straight."

He gave a caustic laugh that in no way even came close to the way he was feeling. "All I keep thinking about is what if you never came to Mule Hollow."

"But God wouldn't let me stay away. My conscience was heavy and then the fire made me realize that if I had died…" She paused at the memory of how close that had been to becoming a reality. "Leo would have been left seemingly all alone in this world. I knew then that I had to come."

He just watched her, silent.

"If it makes any difference, I did come with the intention of telling you that first day. But you were in such a hurry to leave, and I could tell something wasn't right."

He flinched, knowing she spoke the truth. "You've had several chances since then to tell me." His words were as cool as his heart felt. "He's my *son,* Annie. He's been my son from the moment he was conceived, and yet I didn't get the opportunity to be his father."

"I'm sorry, Colt. I truly am. I never understood my sister. Never understood what drove her to throw herself at men like you—" She turned white at her words. Words that hit their mark.

"No need to look shocked. I've honestly done some soul searching since Jess and Luke told me all of their suspicions. And I'm not very proud of my behavior. I would change things if I could."

"We need to look at the future now. The past can't be changed. How do you want to tell Leo?"

Colt's heart ached. He'd thought long and hard about this and knew that he wasn't worthy to let Leo call him Daddy. There were two children dead because of him. He didn't deserve the happiness he'd felt when he'd learned of Leo. He wasn't deserving of such a gift.

"We're not going to tell him."

Annie couldn't believe what he was saying; it was written in her expression.

"I'm going to start being financially responsible for him. I'll pay for his needs and eventually catch up for all the child support that I should have been paying."

"What do you mean, not tell him?"

Colt stalked off the porch away from her. Telling himself with each step to remain steady, that this was the only way to do this. "He deserves better than me."

"I wouldn't have told you if I didn't think you were a good man. I'm sorry, but that's just the way it is. Even though I felt God leading me here. I couldn't do it—couldn't tell you until I saw for myself that you were a good man. And you are. I don't understand why you are refusing your son."

The sun hammered down on them, and a trickle of sweat rolled down his temple. He swiped it away impatiently. "This is the way it's going to be, Annie. I'm going to let you continue to be his guardian. Things will remain like they are except you'll have my financial support."

Annie's eyes flashed. "That's it? That doesn't make sense. What gives you the right to deny him this?"

"What gave you the right to deny him this in the first place?" His jaw clenched and he glared at her, furious. "I've missed six years of my son's life because of you and your sister, and now you want to judge *my* decision to stay out of the picture?"

"Why? That's all I'm asking. You acted like you were mad, but now you refuse to tell him. Colt, you will make a wonderful father. And Leo adores you. Jennifer did make certain of that. You have to give her that much."

Colt knew the truth. He wasn't worthy to be called anyone's hero, much less their father.

He reached in his pocket and pulled out the check he'd written. "Take this."

She stared at it. "I didn't come here for that," she scoffed. "We are doing fine. I came here for you. Leo needs his daddy and, as he grows, he will need you more."

"Use the money and leave it at that." He crossed to his truck, passing Annie on the way. She glared at him. He glared right back at her. She didn't have to understand his reasoning. He was making his choice this time, not her and not her sister.

And not God.

Annie almost crumbled the check into a ball. Almost threw it at Colt's feet, she was so angry with him. Instead she clutched it in her fist and waited for him to leave. Good riddance. The man was good at leaving. Her head spun with the disbelief at what he'd just told her.

Angry and confused, she stuffed the check into her purse and drove back to the clinic just down the road from the ranch. Colt was ahead of her, though she hadn't left his house until after he'd disappeared from view, and she could see his truck now in the distance as she pulled into the gravel parking lot of the clinic.

Walking into the office, Annie came face-to-face with Gabi, coming through the double doors from the back of the building.

"I gather by the look on your face that your meeting with Colt didn't go well," Gabi said, her eyebrows knitting together.

"That man really, really gets my dander up," Annie grumbled, not feeling charitable at all. "He's a pigheaded, stubborn man and I don't understand him *at all!*"

Gabi took a deep breath. "Whew, I guess it didn't go too well."

"At the very least," Annie huffed. "I mean really, I give the guy what I think he wants to hear and then he…" Staring at Gabi, Annie shook her head. "Gabi, I really need some advice here, and you or Montana are the two perfect people for me to confide in. You're his soon-to-be sister-in-law and Montana's already family. That makes you and Montana Leo's aunts. That makes this your business, too."

Gabi's lips flattened into a firm line and she nodded, acknowledging what Annie was certain she'd already figured out. "We thought so," Gabi said quietly. "He doesn't really look like Colt, but despite that, when you look at him, he looks like a miniature Colt. It's because of their build and their mannerisms. When I first saw him I thought he looked familiar, that I knew another little boy that he reminded me of. But then while you were standing here talking, he made a face about something and stuck the tip of his tongue out, and it slammed into me that it was Colt I was seeing. The same thing happened to Luke and Jess when you first met them."

"I didn't get the similarities until I got here. Not ever having really seen Colt, I had no idea until I saw him." Annie sank into her chair, so thankful that the office was slow today. She sent a thank-you up to the Lord, because she knew He'd had a hand in that somehow. "I never meant to be deceptive. I had only known Colt was Leo's daddy for a year. Jenifer told me when she was dying, but made me promise to keep it a secret. She didn't want to push Leo on someone who didn't want him. I think I see what she was doing now, but I couldn't understand it at first. She didn't really know Colt. She was just infatuated with him and loved the aspect of him being a rodeo champ." Annie wagged her head sadly.

"Getting pregnant with Colt's child—well, my sister was reckless and took chances if she thought she would enjoy herself. My conscience bothered me all year. Nearly dying in the fire made me realize that if I hadn't made it out, Leo would have been left thinking he had no one. Not to mention the fact that Colt should be given the opportunity to know his son. I started looking for jobs in Mule Hollow immediately. Gabi, I came here to tell Colt, not to hide it from him."

"I believe you. I just didn't understand. Wow, Annie, you almost died in a fire? That's horrible."

Annie nodded. "It was just a calamity of errors. If a search-and-rescue team member hadn't come by, seen my car running in the drive and hurried to check my place out again, I'd have probably burned out back in my storage room." Annie shivered thinking about it. "I had gone back to our house after the evacuation notice was served and was grabbing what I could. Leo was safe at day care. We were given only a few minutes' notice, but since my home and the landscape company I worked for were in the same area I had time to get home to save pictures and a few of Leo's favorite things. Only, I went out back to grab a box of pictures and some stuff of Jennifer's he would want one day. The door stuck and trapped me inside."

Gabi gasped. "The door just wouldn't open?"

"No. Nothing I did would open it. And there were no windows in the small building. It was horrible. I could smell the smoke getting closer and closer and it was filling up the room. I didn't think I was going to get out. I prayed for God to help me and He did— He sent some-one to open the door. That's the only explanation I have."

"That's amazing. I'm so thankful."

"Colt doesn't want to tell Leo that he's his daddy," Annie blurted out. "I've faced a lot on my own, but I re-ally do need some advice and insight about what to do. Why would Colt want that? I mean, this morning when he walked across the pastures to confront me, he seemed like he was furious that he hadn't had the opportunity to be Leo's daddy. But then he just handed me a check and told me he was going to be financially responsible but that was it. Something about not being worthy to be called Leo's hero, much less his daddy."

Annie's frustrations hadn't let up and the words were just rattling from her. Gabi patiently waited and listened, then spoke.

"He thinks he should have died in that car accident, not the Everson family. Especially those two children. Colt's been messed up really bad, Annie. Jess and Luke have been extremely worried about him. It's almost as if he's had nothing to live for. He's been holed up out there all this time, and that day you saw him at the office was kind of an intervention. They were trying to get him to snap out of his dazed, emotional state of mind. Like you, when you were stuck in that shed, we've been praying for God to help Colt. You and Leo have been so good for him. He came to Montana's for dinner with all of us last night and he seemed like he was in a better place than he's been in a long time."

Annie's blood pressure came down a few points as remorse hit her. "I lost sight of what he'd been through.

I can't even begin to understand the emotions that come with being involved in a tragedy like that."

"Maybe he just needs time. Time and prayer. I know God's got a plan. And despite what Colt is feeling right now, he wasn't responsible for what happened. And even if he was, despite what he believes, everyone is redeemable in God's eyes. I don't think Colt believes that."

Annie was stunned. "Oh, Gabi, how could I have overlooked the need he must have to overcome what had happened in his life?" The reality that this wasn't just about her and Leo sank in. Colt was struggling, and she kept forgetting that he had some major things to deal with besides the sudden appearance of a son. Annie asked God to forgive her for her shortsighted selfishness.

Annie was still praying off and on when she picked Leo up at day care. For this child's sake she prayed all things would work out for the best.

Annie was determined she would do whatever it took to help the situation work out right. In her mind, that was for Leo to know Colt Holden was his daddy.

"I got a big red star on my paper today. I colored a big ol' fat donkey with me riding her! Annie Aunt, you ever in your whole life seen anything as cute as that fat ol' Samantha?" Leo asked as he climbed into his car seat in the back. Annie laughed. She loved this kid. What in the world would her life be like without him? What a blessing he was.

Maybe, just maybe, Leo was here to rescue his daddy.

The thought slipped into her head as she drove home

listening to Leo's lively chatter about his day. *Is that what this is about?* She wasn't going to let him off that easy and say yes…not when she'd once been the kid whose parents had dropped her off on a doorstep and driven away. She knew too well what it felt like not to be wanted. The memory was etched into her soul in bright red. The one thing she hadn't wanted was for Leo to ever feel that he wasn't wanted.

But what she couldn't ever do as long as there was breath in her lungs was forget what her parents had done…and she prayed that one day Leo didn't hold against her what she'd done in keeping his father a secret for a year. But she couldn't dwell on that. No, she just had to fix it. She had to get Colt to claim his son.

"I'm here to work," Colt said without preamble when he walked into the office to face his brothers. It wasn't going to be a pretty meeting.

Luke was sitting behind his desk with a logbook in front of him. Jess was pouring a cup of coffee. He looked as surprised as Luke about Colt showing up.

"It's good to see you coming around," Jess said.

Luke studied him. "You up to working?"

"I'm up for it. I'll be here for a few weeks anyway, until I can find a job." To this point, he'd relied on his earnings as a bull rider to provide his portion of support for the ranch. Jess had a trucking business and Luke had a rodeo stock business. They were building up the new ranch stock and not taking income from it.

Both his brothers were clearly baffled—he didn't blame them.

"What about your bull riding?" Luke said. "You'll be

good as new when that arm is healed, and you might still be in contention for the championship. Your points are high enough that you may not lose a foothold."

"It all depends on if the job I get will let me go compete that week. But I'm not too sure I'll remain up there for long."

"If you ride some before then, you know you will." Jess's brows knitted together. "What's going on?"

"Yeah, Colt. You know we're behind your riding one hundred percent," Luke said.

"Y'all were right," he admitted. "Leo is mine." He'd been fighting the joy that thinking about Leo brought him. With that surge of joy also came the reminder that he had no right to it.

"Man," Jess said. "That's awesome and unbelievable at the same time."

"I was pretty sure," Luke said, disbelief in his voice. "But telling myself I wasn't right at the same time. How are you doing?"

"I'm angry." Colt paced the room, rubbing the back of his neck to ease the knot of tension throbbing there. "I have a child and nobody thought it was my business to be told." He glared at the ceiling, words stuck in his throat. "It stinks."

Both brothers agreed.

"So, what did Annie say?" Luke asked.

He told them the story. They listened intently, and he felt justified in his feelings as he watched their expressions mirror the emotions that were warring inside him.

When he was done talking, Luke's brown eyes held his. "Colt, I love you, brother, but I'm going to say this because I need to know your thoughts. You fathered a child with a woman you didn't know. I'm not sure if you should have expected anything."

"Don't think I don't get that. I messed up. Seems like I've been doing a lot of that lately. If I could go back and change my behavior, I would. But that's not going to change the facts. No, I shouldn't have expected anything. I take full responsibility. But that doesn't change the way I feel. I feel cheated."

"The past is the past," Jess said, his jaw tensed. "What happens now?"

"I start supporting my son. I take financial responsibility for him, and that means I get a job that'll pay those expenses."

Luke looked thoughtful. "How did he take the news that you're his dad?"

"I haven't told him."

"When are you going to do that?" Luke prodded him.

Colt took a deep breath and prepared for the worst. "I'm not."

Jess cocked his head to the side and his blue eyes narrowed. "Did I hear you right?"

Luke's eyes darkened like muddy waters but he didn't say anything, just waited for Colt to explain himself. He had known they wouldn't understand. "You heard me right. I'm taking financial responsibility, but he doesn't need to know anything else."

"Yeah, he does." Luke stood, a challenge in his eyes. "That boy is yours, Colt Holden. You fathered him and he deserves to know who his father is. He deserves to wear the Holden name. I don't care if you want him to or not, you need to take responsibility and do the right thing."

Colt had always idolized his oldest brother. Looked up to him as if he was his dad, because for all intents and purposes Luke had been the one to make sure he was fed, clothed and got to school on time. Seeing the disappointment in him caused a rip of regret inside Colt. "It's for the best. I killed that family. I don't deserve to be called a hero, much less Leo's daddy," he said, repeating the words he'd said to Annie. Both brothers glared at him.

"Come on, man," Jess snapped. "What do we have to do to get it through your thick skull that you need to move on? That wreck was a stinkin' horrible tragedy, but I'm tired of tiptoeing around the fact that it wasn't your fault. There wasn't a thing you could have done about it. Do I feel sorry for that family? Yes, I do. But what you're doing is a waste. You're taking on something that isn't yours to carry. You were just as much a victim of that drunk as they were."

Colt clenched his jaw and held Jess's glare. "I didn't expect y'all to understand. The thing is, I don't need you to. I'm here to find out what I should be doing on the ranch while I figure out what my next move is going to be. I have some job opportunities that I've been offered. I just need to decide which is the right one."

Luke had remained silent, sitting back in his chair. Then he said, "Jess is heading out tomorrow and has several loads scheduled over the next few weeks before his wedding. You can take over feeding the cows."

"I'll start this afternoon." He was glad that at least

Luke was holding his opinion to himself. Luke didn't have to say anything for Colt to know he wasn't happy. But, unlike Jess, Luke was staying out of it. At least for now.

Chapter Nine

Annie took Leo to eat at Sam's diner for breakfast on Saturday morning. She'd heard it was a really neat little place and had the best breakfast in the area. She'd also heard about Applegate Thornton and Stanley Orr. Having met them briefly when she and Leo had attended church, she was curious to see them playing checkers, which, to quote Norma Sue and Esther Mae, "was all the two old coots did."

"Aw, wow," Leo gushed the instant they stepped through the doors of the rustic diner. "That smells awesome!"

Annie's stomach growled at the scent of eggs and bacon and sweet molasses wafting from the kitchen. At a nearby table a cowboy was coating a tall stack of pancakes with thick syrup. There was no mistaking what Leo was going to order the instant they sat down.

"Howdy there, little lady and little fella," Stanley said, sitting across from the thin, dour-faced Applegate. "Y'all come fer some of Sam's home cookin'?"

"Yes sir, Mr. Stanley." Leo had made fast friends with

the plump-faced, good-natured man. "We come to get some pancakes."

"They're good, ain't that right, App?"

"Yup," App grunted, studying the checkerboard with scowling eyes.

Leo walked over and stuffed his fists to his hips as he studied the checkerboard. App turned his head, and he and Leo were almost at eye level. Annie hid a smile when App's frown tilted upward—it was impossible to ignore Leo's bright-eyed curiosity.

"You like checkers?" App asked Leo.

"I don't play 'em," Leo said. "But you play 'em good."

Stanley chuckled. "App wishes."

Annie took a seat in the booth across from App and Stanley. Leo climbed into the seat across from her and placed his elbows on the table. "Man, don't them pancakes smell good!"

Sam came out of the kitchen. He was about four foot nine, bowlegged and wrinkled all over. He had a grin that reached in deep, and warm eyes shining from his well-weathered face. "I learned ta make my pancakes from my granddaddy, and since I was eatin' those pancakes before I was yor age, I can vouch fer the recipe."

"What'll you have?" Sam asked Annie.

"I'll just have a plate of bacon and eggs and some toast. From what I hear, you fix a mean egg."

"The meanest. Orange juice for ya both?"

"Sounds wonderful."

"We're glad y'all have come ta town," Stanley said, jumping App's checker with one of his own.

App frowned. "Shor are. We hear Colt had ta save y'all from a mad momma cow the other mornin'."

"He sure did." Leo beamed, happy to talk about his favorite subject. "He jumped a fence and ran that mean ol' cow plumb off."

Annie had been trying not to think about Colt for the last couple of days. The man had reasons for not wanting to tell Leo he was his daddy, and she'd been trying to justify his actions with those reasons. But she just kept coming up short. Try as she might, Annie couldn't let him off that easy. After all, he'd seen Leo. Knew what a great kid he was and still turned his back on him. She'd known all her life what it felt like to know her parents hadn't wanted her or her sister. She just couldn't understand the man...and she couldn't forgive him for what he was doing.

Hearing Leo tell App, Stanley and Sam how wonderful he was made her want to scream. It didn't matter that Colt had just found out about his son. And she'd thought hard about it, and decided it didn't matter if he was hurting from the wreck. Now that he knew about Leo, he should have embraced his son.

Until he acknowledges Leo, she had no respect for the man. None.

The church service was already halfway done when Colt slipped into the back pew beside App. He'd tried hard to talk himself out of coming and he'd almost succeeded. It had been out of honor for the Eversons that he'd come. And to see Leo.

Colt had stayed away from Annie and Leo for almost a week, but it had been hard to do. To his surprise App didn't give him a scowl for his lateness, but instead he grinned and held out his hand for a handshake.

"Good to have you here," he said, his greeting so loud due to his hard hearing that several heads turned his way. Leo was one of them. As if drawn to the little eyes peeking over the pew three rows up, Colt zeroed in on Leo almost instantly.

His son yanked on Annie's shirtsleeve. "Colt's here," he whispered. "I can see him."

"Shhh, Leo, the preacher is about to speak."

Colt pulled his gaze away from the back of Annie's glossy hair. Her shoulders had stiffened when she'd realized he'd sat down somewhere behind her. He knew she wasn't any happier with him than he was with her. She tilted her head slightly and whispered into Leo's ear. Her lips curved into a soft smile as she spoke.

He wasn't here to think about her.

He was here because, since learning he was a father, he'd been rethinking some things about his life. He had no right to feel the pride and joy that he felt thinking about Leo being his child. But he felt it, and with that he also felt a sense of responsibility. He'd not cared if he lived or died since the wreck, but Leo's appearance had given him a reason to start living again. He needed to support his son. He needed to provide a good life for him. He'd come here today not only to search for answers, but also because he wanted to see Leo.

Colt wasn't up to telling Leo who he was yet, but as a man Leo looked up to, Colt knew it was time to step up and meet that challenge in a positive way. Coming to church was a step in the right direction.

Did it matter that he had lost confidence in God's reasoning? That was a question Colt couldn't answer right now. Or was it more important to be here, showing Leo that he did have faith? Shaky faith right now, but faith all the same.

Chance Turner, a former bull rider and rodeo preacher, was now the pastor of the tiny church. He met Colt's gaze from the pulpit and gave him a tip of his head and a smile. Colt knew that Chance understood some of what he was feeling. Colt had talked with him when he'd first come home after being stomped by the bull. He'd urged Colt to hang on to his faith with his fingernails if that was what it took, but not to turn his back on God. That was what Colt was trying to do. His fingernails felt broken and bleeding at times—it was so hard to cling to something when there seemed to be nothing to latch on to. What God had allowed to happen was still impossible to understand.

But he was here. Hoping God was trying to hang on to him just as hard.

"Heya, Colt," Leo called the minute the church service ended and everyone started moving from their pews and heading outside.

Annie watched helplessly as Leo shot past her and chased after Colt's rigid form. All she could do was follow the crowd out into the sunlight and the inevitable meeting. She'd struggled to listen to Pastor Chance the entire service, because she knew this meeting was coming soon after Adela began playing the benediction.

"Colt, you're a sight for sore eyes," Norma Sue said, barreling into Colt's path—halting his forward movement and causing Annie's insides to knot. There was no way Norma Sue and Esther Mae had made it down the aisle that fast. Nope, the two ladies must have spotted

Colt, busted out the side door and raced down the sidewalk in order to cut him off at the pass, in order to stop him before he reached the parking lot.

"Coming out to visit you has been heavy on our minds," Esther Mae said, patting his arm and grinning. "We just can't let a strong, good-hearted cowboy like you waste away out there, so we were going to bring you some food this afternoon."

Leo was beaming up at them like a beacon of fluorescent light that matched the canary-yellow dress Esther Mae wore. Annie couldn't very well walk on by and make a run for her car—no matter how much the thought appealed to her. *Waste away*—Annie caught those words and her eyes zeroed in on the hard biceps Esther Mae had hold of. The man was brokenhearted and hardheaded, but he was surely not wasting away. Yes, he was thinner than his pictures but not withered…not by a long shot. The thought almost had her tripping over her own feet, but she managed to stumble to a halt right before she reached them. She tore her eyes off where they'd locked on to his biceps and instantly met Colt's stare. A heated blush rose up, stinging her cheeks at the realization that he'd caught her staring at his muscles. It wasn't as if she hadn't seen a man's muscles before.

The twinkle in Esther Mae's eye told Annie that the matchmaking posse hadn't missed her interest in Colt, either. Literally swallowing a groan, Annie thought things couldn't possibly get any worse—until Leo proved her wrong.

"Colt, I want to learn to ride a bull. And I want *you* to teach me."

Annie choked, coughing real hard and wheezing in

just enough air to inflate her suddenly airless windpipes. "No…" she sputtered, looking from Leo to Colt.

As if to reassure her, Colt's eyes softened when they met hers. "That's not something a little boy your age needs to think about right now."

"Why not? I want to learn to ride like you."

She hadn't considered this until now, and her fear of it must have shown in her face, because everyone began telling Leo why he was too young to even think about riding a bull.

"Can you teach me to rope then? I really wanna learn. *Please,*" Leo begged.

Colt swallowed hard, meeting her glare. Her stomach turned over looking at him, and her anger at him not admitting that he was Leo's dad shot it through the roof. Did that stop the hard-nosed man from toying with his child? Oh no, it did not.

"Sure," he said in the next breath. "I can teach you to do that."

If the whole town, and especially the sharp-eyed posse, hadn't been milling about, Annie might have stomped his toe with the heel of her shoe. Instead she clamped her mouth shut, and locked her arms across her middle, instead of punching him in the arm.

"That sounds like a plan, little man." Norma Sue slapped Colt on the shoulder. "Colt might make his fame and fortune on the backs of bulls, but he used to make a lot of rodeo winnings roping, too."

"Can you teach me today?" Leo persisted. "I can come over and we can practice on your roping dummy."

Annie wanted to protest, but before she could get so

much as a squeak out, Colt was telling Leo that coming
to his house sounded like a great plan.

Annie wanted to hit the man with her purse.

"What time should they be there?" Esther Mae asked,
shocking Annie by her question.

"Yes," Norma Sue added. "We'll bring our casseroles
out either before or after y'all have your roping lesson,
so that we don't get in y'all's way."

Lacy Matlock, who'd been in conversation with another group of ladies, walked over toward Annie. She'd
obviously overheard the conversation going on between
Colt and the ladies and Leo, because her blue eyes were
twinkling with mirth.

"You know what's going on, don't you?" she whispered, a grin spread across her friendly expression.
"They've found their new match. And it looks good
from all of our viewpoints."

Annie's mouth fell open. "A match," she gasped in a
strangled whisper, turning to Lacy. "But what do I do?"
She didn't need the ever-persistent matchmaking posse
of Mule Hollow latching on to the idea of her and Colt
as a possible love match! It stole her breath, even as an
unwanted tremor of awareness swept through her.

"Not sure there is anything to do but be aware of
what's going on. I have to say, though, that you and
Leo seem to be bringing Colt back to life. And that has
nothing whatsoever to do with the posse's shenanigans."

Annie opened her mouth to say something, then
thought better of it and clamped her lips tight. She
couldn't tell anyone that Leo being his son was affecting Colt this way. "He likes Leo," she whispered ur-
gently. "It has absolutely nothing to do with me. *Nothing*.

Why, we fight most of the time." She was ready to fight the man right now.

Lacy chuckled. "That's called sparks—and the posse can spot a spark from miles away." She winked and went back to her prior conversation, leaving Annie frustrated.

Annie's stomach roiled furiously in denial. But she knew some of it was true. At least on her part. But sparks or no sparks, disagreeing about Leo put out any fires that the sparks might cause.

She turned back to the conversation. Colt's warm brown eyes met hers and Annie felt as if she were melting inside.

Suddenly she knew she was in big trouble in more ways than one. Because this was not at all what she wanted to feel. But she did.

It was a perfect summer day—if you called ninety degrees in the shade perfect. And Colt did, especially since he had Leo standing beside him in his yard.

"That's good, Leo," Colt said, watching Leo's loop fly toward the roping dummy six feet away.

"I can do better," Leo said when it missed. With determination in his voice, he pulled his rope back and coiled it as Colt had shown him.

His son had a good eye, great coordination and an insatiable persistence to be good at what he did. At his young age, if harnessed and focused it could take him far. Pride warmed through him like sunlight rolling from behind a cloud. *My son.*

"You keep practicing. I'm going to go over there and talk to your aunt for a few minutes. Is that all right?"

"Sure it is. Annie Aunt looks kinda sad today. I don't think she wanted to come watch me chunk this rope."

Colt had noticed the way Annie looked, though, and it wasn't sadness that he was seeing. It was pure and simple anger. She'd been cold to him ever since he'd given her that check and told her he wanted his identity kept secret.

She stiffened when he sank to the steps beside her. He needed to get some decent outdoor chairs for the small porch, but he'd been fine sitting on the steps when he came outside. A woman would like a chair, he figured— not that Annie planned to be coming over all the time. He had a feeling Leo had been absolutely correct when he'd said she hadn't wanted to come.

She scooted away from him on the step, and it was all he could do not to move closer to her. He'd been thinking of Annie a lot. As much as he'd been thinking about his newfound son. There was no denying that he was mad at her, purely aggravated that she'd kept his son from him. But late into the night, when sleep evaded him and he'd been sitting here on this very step listening to the sounds of the forest at 2:00 a.m., he'd admitted to himself it was more. Annie drew him; something about her spoke to the unrest in his soul.

"Annie, look at me," he said when she was content to watch Leo throw his rope, keeping her eyes purposefully straight ahead. "Look, I know you're not happy with me."

"You got that right," she said, her gaze darting at him for a brief but sharp moment. "I'm looking at a man who is passing up on the best thing this world has to offer. Look at him. He's your son and you won't acknowledge that."

He felt her intense anger directed at him. Colt fought down the guilt that clawed at him. "I'm glad Leo has you," he said. "Annie, I can't expect you to understand my reasoning. I'm not even asking you to. There was a moment that I almost…" He looked down at the rough wood beneath his boots. He couldn't tell her that he couldn't acknowledge Leo as his because of what he'd done. He didn't deserve Leo. "Telling Leo is just not an option. Maybe at one time it would have been. But I'm glad he has you."

"You don't get it. What if something were to happen and he didn't have me anymore? Who would he have?"

"In that case he would have me. He has me now, just not in name."

"Y'all, look at me," Leo called, grinning when his rope landed on the nose of the roping dummy.

"Lookin' good," Annie called, giving him a thumbs-up while Colt called out his approval, too.

"You're doing great, buddy, keep it up," he said, watching Leo coil his rope and then start twirling it over his head again. When he looked at Annie, she was watching him with curious, sad eyes.

"Does it have something to do with the wreck and that family? The ones who died?"

Locking down hard on his molars, his jaw jerked. "Yeah, it does," he found himself admitting. "How could it not?"

They stared at each other for a long, silent moment. He knew there was nothing he could do to explain what was going on inside him. Annie's beautiful eyes searched deep, as if she were trying hard to figure it out on her own.

She sighed and her features, taut with anger since her arrival, relaxed. "Then, that's the way it'll be," she said, and then she smiled. "One day, when you've moved past the grief that's tearing you up inside, maybe you'll change your mind. Until then, I'll love him and be his family and you'll be there for him. You'll be the man in his life. Right?"

Her kindness surprised him. Grief, she'd called it. He couldn't deny that was exactly what it was.

"I think you've had a hard life, Colt Holden. And in a way, so have I. I think we both agree that we want to make Leo's young years more normal and secure than either of ours were."

"Yes," he said, captured by her words and her voice, so soft and sure, Colt could listen to her speak for the rest of his life. The knowledge seeped through him, warming his heart. *You'll be the man in his life.* Her words about Leo rang in his head and Colt wondered, who would be the man in Annie's life?

Smiling, she held out her hand. "Truce? Together we'll make his childhood healthy and happy."

Colt didn't hesitate in taking her hand. Her fingers slid easily into his and locked with his in a handshake they both meant with all their hearts.

They were sitting on his step holding hands and smiling at each other when Norma Sue's big double-cab truck came growling through the trees.

He'd picked up on what was going on at church that morning. Norma Sue and Esther Mae had set their sights on matching him up, and he'd known the instant that focus had zeroed in on him and Annie. Seeing them like this was going to do nothing but fan the flames of interest.

Pulling away, Colt stood and moved toward the truck He wasn't going to linger on the porch beside Annie and give them any more to talk about than what he'd already given them.

Only problem with that was, after looking into Annie's eyes and holding her hand, he'd given *himself* too much to think about!

Chapter Ten

Annie stared at herself in the mirror and felt a jangle of nerves. Nonsense, she told herself, wishing with all her might that the thought of spending the evening with Colt didn't make her pulse beat faster and her nerves rattle so. But nonsense or not, it was the truth.

The worst part was everyone seemed to be hoping— even praying—that she and Colt would fall in love.

It was enough to make a woman who had no plans to fall for the good-looking bull rider scream. It was the perfect situation, they all thought…her being Leo's aunt and Colt being Leo's hero. And dad. Though they weren't saying, Annie knew that the posse had their suspicions about the relationship between Leo and Colt. The more time the two spent together, the more time folks had to realize how much they resembled each other in so many ways. Speculation was rampant, and though nothing was being said to her directly, she could see it and feel it when she was around. Then again, it could be her mind going crazy on her like always. Colt's family had all figured it out, and though their speculations had been confirmed by Colt, they'd been sworn to keep to themselves what they knew. No one else had had their suspicions confirmed. Not even Colt's mother, whom Annie had yet to meet. But Colt had told Annie he'd rather not bring that complication into the picture right now. She didn't know exactly what that meant.

"He's coming, he's coming!" Leo called as he came racing into her bedroom with a big grin on his face. "Are you ready to go?"

Despite her nerves, Annie had to laugh. "Yes, I'm ready."

"Then come on." Leo grabbed her hand and tugged her down the hall. "We got a rodeo to get to."

The third and final Mule Hollow Homecoming Rodeo was tonight and they were going with Colt. There had been one a month over the summer. The ladies of Mule Hollow had come up with the idea to try and get some of the folks who'd moved away from the small town to come home for a visit and maybe decide the little town was worth moving back to. Though Annie wasn't exactly sure what all the fuss was about, since the town had been growing one marriage after another for the last few years.

Leo let go of her hand and threw open the front door just as Colt was walking up the steps. Annie fought off the butterflies that swarmed inside her chest at the sight of the man. He carried himself with such control. Though he wasn't quite six foot, he seemed larger than life. It was a trait of a bull rider, she'd come to realize. Maybe it was because they weren't afraid to get on the back of a two-thousand-pound bull that would love to pound them into the ground. Annie figured if she could do that and come out alive, then she might carry herself with that much pride. But even if she tried to carry herself the way Colt did, there just wasn't any way it would look good on her. He definitely took her breath away. Especially tonight. He wore a starched black Western shirt with lots of stitching and pearl snaps. His jeans were dark and well fitted, and the buckle he wore was huge and sparkled with the intricate detail and small stones crafted into the silver creation.

"Wow, what a buckle!" Leo exclaimed.

Colt chuckled, and the sound warmed something deep in Annie's chest.

"It's one of my buckles from the finals. You'll have one of these one day if you keep practicing like you're doing."

"I know it," Leo chirped, as if winning was a piece of cake.

"You look nice," Colt said, his gaze sweeping over to Annie.

Instantly her blood warmed and her skin tingled. "Thank you." She suddenly felt self-conscious about the fact that she'd actually fussed over her appearance because she was going to spend the evening with him.

"She sure does." Leo beamed. "I didn't think she was ever gonna figure out what to wear."

Colt grinned. "She changed clothes a bunch?" he asked, his eyes teasing.

Leo's face scrunched with disbelief. "At least a hundred times. You should see all the clothes stacked on her bed."

Annie gasped. "Leo, it's not that bad."

Judging by the grin plastered on his face, Colt was

enjoying this. Annie knew good and well that he was thinking she'd done all that changing because of him.

Annie could still feel the warmth of his hand from a week ago when they'd shaken hands and agreed to give Leo a better life than they'd had. Annie had buried herself in her Bible since that day. She'd felt lost the moment she'd looked into his eyes and wondered what it would be like if they were in love, if they were a family.

The idea filled her with feelings she couldn't explain. But one of those feelings was fear. All her life she'd dreamed of love. She'd craved it, but she couldn't let down the walls that she'd built around her heart. And here she was looking at Colt Holden, and suddenly all the hopes and wants seemed to fill her up inside to the point where she thought she might explode. It terrified her.

"Can I ride Samantha?" Leo asked as they walked through the small fair that was set up outside the covered rodeo arena. Lilly and Cort Wells, looking like the cutest couple in the world, her with her head of dark, tight ringlets and he the serious-looking horse trainer. He was intent at the moment to corral the herd of kids swarming around them looking to pet the animals and take a spin on Samantha or a couple of miniature ponies they had brought along.

Their son, Joshua, who was about four, waved Leo over to where he was feeding a baby calf a bottle. "Wanna feed him?" Joshua asked. "He don't mind."

"Sure," Leo said, and jumped right into the task.

"He's game for anything, isn't he?" Colt said.

"Oh, if you only knew the half of it. That little boy can get into more mischief. Jennifer and I held our breath many times worrying what he was going to do next. But what am I supposed to expect? She brought him up idolizing riding bulls."

"You wouldn't have done that, would you?"

"Jennifer and I didn't see eye to eye on a lot of things."

He had figured that out without her telling him. From what he could remember about Jennifer, she was highstrung and had enjoyed partying pretty heavily. The truth was, she'd chased him hard from rodeo to rodeo. He wasn't proud of his own actions, but he knew that if he hadn't been stuck out on the road, he wouldn't have been attracted to Jennifer. Annie was different from her sister. She was quieter and he knew that playing the field wasn't something a woman like Annie would even consider. Following rodeo cowboys around for the fun of it wasn't anywhere near her radar.

He had a feeling that Annie Ridgeway was a one-man woman. He liked that. He liked it a lot.

Not that what he liked mattered. They were in this odd relationship strictly because of Leo. Keeping his mind off Annie was the best policy. Besides that, he knew letting himself think about looking for love, for happiness, was a lost cause for him.

Samantha walked over and nudged Leo, then pulled her big lips back and grinned. Leo and Joshua laughed.

"He's making friends," Colt said, trying to make himself not notice how the sun made Annie's hair shimmer like warm spun gold.

"Yes, I'm so glad. Joshua is a little younger, but there's several boys his age. He'll have a great group to go to school with next year." She inhaled as she nodded. "I'm really glad we moved here, Colt."

Before they'd shown up, he'd been on the verge of falling apart. Now he had a reason to get up in the morning. A reason to try and move forward, to come to terms with the tragedy he'd caused. "I am, too."

Two hours later, Colt shifted his sling and wished his collarbone wasn't broken. Thankfully, it was almost healed, but he wished he could be out there on the back of a bull competing with the rest of the bull riders, who were gearing up for their time in the arena. It would be easier than sitting beside Annie in a crowd of people who were causing the back of his neck to itch from all the watchful eyes keeping tabs on them!

Sitting so close to her in the crowded arena stands, their legs and shoulders rubbing with every movement, he couldn't think straight. And he was working hard to keep his head on target and answer the constant string of questions that Leo kept firing at his distracted brain.

Colt hadn't wanted to come to the rodeo. He'd dreaded everything about it except being with Leo. For an injured bull rider, sitting in the stands watching was torture. Compound that with the guilt he felt for enjoying life, then tack on to that sitting beside Annie. Annie, who made him feel alive just being around her—yes sir, he was being tortured in more ways than one.

"I'm gonna do that one day. I am," Leo stated, pointing at the ropers as they busted from the gate and charged after the calf. Leo clapped and hooted when the cowboy's rope caught the calf; his horse stopped running, the cowboy jumped from its back and ran to the calf. "Look, look, look!" Leo exclaimed, pointing at the roper, who threw the calf to its back, yanked the pig string from between his lips and expertly wrapped three of the calf's legs together before throwing his hands up in the air, signaling the timer to stop. "Man oh man, I am gonna do that one day." Leo whirled around, his face an electric show of excitement.

Colt laughed, his heart full of love. He wanted more than anything to hug his son tight and tell him he was his daddy. And he loved him. That he would help him achieve any dream he wanted. As a child, that had been something Colt had never known.

He'd told himself all his life that it didn't matter. He'd gone on and fought for his dreams without the support of his alcoholic father or his mother, who'd left because she hadn't been able to handle the life she'd been dealt. Only trying recently to come back into their lives. Looking at Leo, he knew he'd do anything to make sure Leo felt loved and secure. *But will you tell him you're his daddy?*

"I'd much rather you learn that than bull riding," Annie said, making no bones about the fact that bulls scared her and she was not going to go down without a fight where Leo was concerned.

"I'm gonna learn that, too. I'm gonna be as good as Colt."

Colt could feel Annie tensing up beside him. "I have a feeling you'll be better than me," Colt said to Leo. Then to Annie, he added, "Relax. Bull riding is technique and self-control. By the time I turn Leo loose, he'll have both and there will be no stopping him."

"That's right, no stopping me. I'm gonna be the best there ever was."

Annie laughed at that despite the tension he could see in every fiber of her body. "*That* I have no doubt about." She snatched his cowboy hat from his head and ruffled his hair affectionately. "You're just stubborn enough to do it."

"And to be great it will take every ounce of stubbornness to pull it off."

"Are you stubborn?" Leo asked, leaning his hip against Colt's knee and resting his hand on Colt's leg.

Colt felt a contentment he'd never felt before looking at the relaxed way Leo had around him. God had blessed him with this child. The realization thundered through Colt. "I'm stubborn. When I know what I want, I go after it. You'll be the same."

Leo grinned. "You betcha."

"Leo, do you want to go to the concession stand with us?" Norma Sue called from the aisle. Adela was beside her, a sweet smile lighting her brilliant blue eyes—eyes Colt thought probably looked brighter because her short white hair was such a contrast. Just as her being so dainty and gentle contrasted with Norma Sue, and her robust figure and even larger personality. How those two were such close friends had always baffled Colt growing up, and even more so now. But they were. And it worked. Add Esther Mae into the mix and it was like adding fizz to a root beer float.

"Can I, Annie Aunt? Can I?" Leo spun toward Annie and asked.

"Sure you can." Annie smiled. "Thanks for asking him," she called down the row to the ladies. They were grinning.

"I might take him up to the announcer's booth, if you don't mind. My Roy Don would enjoy showing him the show from up there."

"Sure," Annie said as Leo whooped and started toward the posse.

Colt watched Leo scoot through the crowd toward the ladies and realized that he and Annie were alone. They were in a crowd, but suddenly with no buffer. "Do you want me to get you something from the concession stand?" he offered.

She shook her head. "No, I'm fine."

They sat like that for a few minutes, feeling like strangers. Colt's leg burned where her jeans-clad leg touched his. Colt struggled to figure out what to talk to her about. "You're sure, because I can go."

A smile tugged at her lips. "And mess up Leo's independence? I don't think so. We'll just sit here and chill."

"Okay," he grunted, feeling awkward. "He's a great kid, Annie."

"Yes, he is," she answered, and then silence landed between them again. "Is this driving you crazy—not being out there?" she asked at last.

"Yeah, I'd be lying if I said it didn't." He shrugged a shoulder. "But it's not the same anymore." He looked at the bull riders beginning to mill around behind the gates. "So much has happened in the last month that it feels like years."

"Word on the street is you're thinking about not competing in the finals." She gave a shy smile. "And yes, I listened to the talk about you. I have to admit to being curious about Leo's…" Her voice trailed off and she glanced around. "Well, you know," she finished.

The spark of interest that she would listen died when he realized it was because she was curious about him only as Leo's daddy. It was just as well. He knew she was interested; he could see it in her eyes. But since she didn't like him, and was basically only tolerating him because of the situation, what had he expected?

"Yeah, I know. Look, I've got a lot on my mind. A lot to figure out."

"I know that. I'm trying to be patient like we discussed. Are you willing to talk?"

He studied her, considering her offer. "It's not that easy."

"I'm sure it isn't. You've been through a lot. I understand that." She looked away toward the first bull rider lowering himself onto the bull's back. "I just thought if you needed someone to talk to… But I know you have your brothers. Your family. Having a family is nice."

The crowd around them went wild as they watched the five seconds it took for the rider to be thrown to the ground. The bull fighters raced out and distracted the hulking bull as the unhurt cowboy jogged to the fence.

"There are some things no one can fix." He hesitated and then, looking into the compassion of her eyes, he continued. "A family gone can't be brought back. The hole their absence makes in the lives of their loved ones and friends can't be fixed."

Around them the stands erupted as Roy Don announced the next bull by name and the cowboy riding him, too. Colt didn't even look—he was too busy looking at Annie's sad expression.

"You're right about that. My house mother at the last foster home I was in always said that God had a plan. No matter if we could see it or not, He had a plan. I tell myself that all the time. I think it's something you really need to grasp. We may never know why this tragedy happened. But no matter how much you wished it was you who died instead of the Eversons, it won't change the fact. You need to come to terms with that. You don't have to like it…but you have to accept it."

"Colt!" Leo called as he wove his way through the people sitting on the stadium bench. Colt hadn't realized Leo was coming up the steps, he'd been too focused on his conversation with Annie. Annie looked just as startled as he was.

"What is it?" he asked, reaching out to steady his son as he scrunched past the last set of knees.

Breathless with excitement, Leo grinned at Colt and Annie. "There's gonna be a rodeo just for little kids like me! Can you *believe* it? A six-year-old like *me.*"

"Whoa, slow down and breathe," Colt said, grinning.

"Excuse me. Coming through," Norma Sue said, squeezing her way toward them. A bit larger than Leo, she had men standing up and trying to scoot steel benches out of the way with their legs in order to give her the room she needed to get through the crowd. Her elbow hit a cowboy in the head who was sitting one row forward. His Stetson went flying and landed on the lady two rows farther forward. All this during what was supposed to be the ride of the night, by a bull rider who was trying to take Colt down a notch in the national standings!

"Hey," the cowboy boomed, glaring at Norma Sue. Obviously not from around these parts, the poor fellow had *no* idea what he was biting off by glaring at Norma Sue like that.

The robust rancher woman halted in her maneuvers and swirled around to face the unhappy cowboy. Unfortunately for the hospitable fellow who'd stood up to let her through, he was knocked back by her hips as she swung around to face the rude sodbuster. "I didn't mean to knock your hat off, son," she apologized as folks turned to see what was happening.

"You need to watch yourself," the poor, misguided soul began, then halted when Norma Sue stuffed her fist onto her hips and leaned toward him, her expression easily telegraphing her displeasure at his rudeness.

"Did I tell you I was sorry, young man?" she huffed. When he didn't say anything, she hiked a brow and tipped her chin. "Well, did I or didn't I? What, now that you've got an old woman all riled up, you're gonna pipe down?"

"Well, I, I…" He swallowed hard and glanced from side to side, spotting the expressions of irritation and outright humor at his situation.

"That's right. *Now* you're thinking about finding your manners. 'Cause I know your momma probably taught you better. If she didn't, then honey, you've come callin' on the right little gal to set you straight."

Colt almost choked on his own laughter and Annie's shoulders were shaking. Leo looked at Norma Sue with openmouthed amazement.

"That bad man shoulda kept his mouth shut," Leo whispered behind his cupped hand into Colt's ear.

"I reckon that woulda been the best thing to do." Colt chuckled.

"So what do you want to say to me now?" Norma Sue asked, totally fixated on the wish-he-could-crawl-under-a-rock cowboy.

"I'm sorry, ma'am. Didn't mean to get so upset when

you—" He looked down at his boots. "When you were just trying to get past."

Norma Sue relaxed, grinned and reached out and chucked the fellow on the shoulder good-naturedly. "Now, there ya go. Don't you feel better now?" He was shaking in his boots and she was grinning from ear to ear, totally oblivious that she'd just taken an eight-second bull ride to a different level.

"Y'all get on back to your bull-ride watching. The show's over." She scooted the last foot to where they were sitting and squeezed in beside Annie. "Rude folks. Somebody's gotta teach'um some manners."

"Shor do," Leo said, his little face scrunching up with his indignation at the situation. "You did good, Miss Norma Sue."

She smiled. "Thanks, cutie pie. You just remember when you grow up to be a gentleman—that's the real cowboy way. And the Godly way."

"Yes, ma'am. I promise."

"Good, now that that's settled, I was coming to explain about the kiddy rodeo. Annie, I hope you'll consider letting Leo compete."

"Well, I guess that would be fine. He looks like he really wants to. But he doesn't know how to do anything."

"That's nothing," Norma Sue hooted, looking at Colt. "He's got Colt living across the barbed wire from him. Colt can fix him up with anything he wants to do. Can't you, Colt?"

"Yeah, can't you Colt?" Leo added, his entire body wiggling with the prospect of what was to come.

Colt laughed, not about to go against anything Norma

Sue said at this moment. "You and me, kiddo. We'll have you rodeo ready in no time."

"Yup," Norma Sue agreed. "Now, that's what I'm talking about."

"What kind of events will there be?"

"They're gonna have mutton bustin'!"

Colt enjoyed Annie's baffled expression as she turned questioning eyes to him.

"That's kids trying to ride large sheep. Since they're too young to ride steers."

"It's the cutest thing you ever saw," Norma Sue added. "Leo would enjoy it."

The crowd was going wild around them. Everyone stopped talking as their attention turned to the great eight-second ride going on out in the arena. The bull rider was riding the twisting bull and giving it his all. Colt's hand on his good arm fisted into a ball and he recorded in his mind everything that was right about the ride and everything he would have done differently. All in all, the rider did a great job and deserved all the attention his ride had garnered. Though he had been preoccupied with Annie and Leo, Colt figured this was the winning ride of the night.

Leo pumped his little fist in the air. "That was awesome!"

Annie swallowed hard. "Norma Sue, I'll need to think about this mutton bustin'. What else will be at the rodeo?"

"But Annie Aunt!" Leo exclaimed.

"Leo, I said I need to think about this."

"I think it sounds like a fun thing for him to do," Colt

said, not getting the big deal. It was mutton bustin'—
what was the big deal?

The instant Annie's eyebrow shot up and those big
eyes of hers narrowed as they locked on to him said it
all. He'd just made a mistake.

And by the look of things, he wasn't going to fare
much better than the poor whupped-down cowpoke
who'd dared to cross Norma Sue a few minutes earlier.

Chapter Eleven

"We'll discuss this later, Leo," Annie said as she sent Leo to brush his teeth before going to bed. At his protest she shook her head. "Young man, if you want the answer to be no about this rodeo, then keep fussing. I've told you I need more information, and until I get it I'm not going to say yes to mutton bustin'."

He sighed an overly exaggerated sigh. "Yes, ma'am." Trudging down the hall he disappeared into the bathroom.

Annie sighed to herself, her heart heavy with the idea of disappointing Leo. She was here to protect him though, and she planned on researching the events before she let Leo do anything that could jeopardize him. And how dare Colt!

Turning back to the kitchen she went to the sink to wash the dishes that were waiting on her. Time had run out on getting the dinner plates washed when she'd foolishly spent far too long in front of her closet contemplating what outfit to wear to the rodeo. Lost in thought, she ran the hot water into the sink, testing it to get the temperature right as the suds began to grow.

What did Colt expect? That he was going to keep his identity hidden and yet override her decision making? And what had she been thinking—the man was his daddy after all. Pulling him into this did give him rights. However, it didn't seem fair for those rights to include upstaging her decisions.

Annie grabbed a plate, and though all it had held was a turkey sandwich—Leo's favorite—she scrubbed it as if it had dried three-day-old eggs clinging to it. Colt had better be glad he'd taken his cue and gone home the minute he'd dropped them off. She scrubbed harder. He'd better also be glad that she'd held her dissatisfaction to herself, for the most part.

"What was he thinking?" she grumbled as she snapped the water back on and rinsed the sparkling dish beneath the clear warm water.

And here she'd believed they'd made a connection for a minute there—not that she had been sure at all what she was doing, but something had passed between them. Her hands stilled in the dishwater. Colt had a family he could talk to. Unlike her, he had someone to gain insight from in difficult situations. He wasn't like her, relying on herself or nearly complete strangers for advice. Hanging her head, she paused washing the plate. Fighting the mixture of anger and confusion, she gripped the sink and went to the one she did have to talk to…she went to God.

Dear Lord, please help me to know what I'm supposed to do. Please lead me to not make rash decisions. Please calm my spirit and allow me to hear your direction. Your calling.

Finishing the dishes, a sense of calm came over her, just as she'd prayed for. Annie determined that she would trust God to help her make the right choices for Leo. And for herself, she didn't need to think about anything that had to do with her. She needed to concentrate on Leo and let her own needs remain in the background.

As for Colt, God was going to have to give her some direction on how to deal with the man who obviously didn't want to drive the vehicle but was certainly showing signs of being a backseat driver. And if there was one thing Annie didn't like, it was a backseat driver. Either you had your hands on the wheel, ready to take responsibility for the loaded car, or you were just a passenger.

Colt Holden was going to have to figure out whether he wanted up in the front seat if he planned on telling her how to raise her nephew. Until that time, she'd decide things such as whether or not Leo got strapped to the back of a big, fat, fuzzy sheep. Which did seem pretty harmless, but was it mutton bustin' today and bull riding tomorrow?

All roads led to somewhere and she just wasn't sure that was a road she was ready to head down.

Goodness, what in the world had Jennifer been thinking when she'd decided to be infatuated by men who thought nothing about risking their lives on the back of a mean hunk of bull?

Jennifer hadn't been thinking. Nope, and just like everyone else in Annie's life, she'd cut out of the picture early and left all the thinking and the worrying up to Annie. Frustration washed over her like the hot water she had her hands in. Annie's nerves and her patience were worn thin, and her ability to think in a rational, clear manner was disappearing faster than a fresh-baked cherry pie in a roomful of hungry cowboys.

Please, God, please, give me strength.... She bowed her head again, right there at the sink and let the plea of a prayer ring out silently through her soul. *Give me strength and wisdom.* God promised in the Bible that if you asked for wisdom He would give it to you. Look what He'd done for King Solomon. When he'd prayed for wisdom, God had made him the wisest man there ever was.

Of course, with all that wisdom, Solomon had *still* messed up.

Just please give me a little touch of wisdom to help me know how to do what is right for Leo.... And while You're at it, please let me not fall for Colt Holden. Please let me keep my heart intact.

"What do you think?" Gabi asked, aglow in the excitement of showing Annie and Susan her wedding dress. Covered in a clear plastic bag, it hung from the top of the door. White with small ruffles that cascaded down from the knee to the floor, it was sleeveless and the bodice had a wide scoop neck adorned with tiny pearls from shoulder to shoulder.

"It's beautiful," Susan said, awe in her voice as she studied the dress. "And it's going to look even more beautiful on you."

Annie ran her fingers down the plastic, as if she were touching the dress. "Gabi, it's perfect. I love it." Annie loved looking at wedding dresses. As a little girl she'd lain in bed at night in one foster home after another and dreamed that one day she'd marry. Or in those days, infatuated with Cinderella, she dreamed of finding her prince. That he would come and sweep her off her feet and they would be married—she in the perfect dress and he in his perfect tuxedo—and they would live happily ever after in their perfect castle. That had been when she was barely older than Leo. By the time she was fourteen, she and Jennifer had been sent to the girls' ranch, where they finished out their days until the system booted them out into the world on their own. Annie had stopped dreaming of love. She'd closed off her heart and thrown away the key. She'd realized that opening her heart made her vulnerable to pain. Too many people had thought she was not worthy of love. And she certainly wasn't going to find one more person to fall for who could then toss her heart back to her on a platter.

Nope. Annie had gotten over dreaming of her prince and true love...but she couldn't hide her love of wedding dresses. She had a weakness for them.

"Thank y'all. I'm about as excited as a woman can get. I mean, really, I had no idea when I came here that I was going to meet Jess. And here I am."

"Is it going to be a big wedding?" Annie couldn't help asking. She was happy for Gabi and Jess.

Susan and Gabi looked at each other and chuckled. "Who knows? There could be a hundred people there or three hundred. Jess has been inviting everyone. You and Leo are coming, I hope.... Maybe Colt can escort you."

Annie went on alert. "I don't think so. Besides, isn't Colt in the wedding? He'll be too busy, I'm sure."

A truck drove up outside. "Lunch break is over." Susan grinned. "You'd better put that somewhere safe, Gabi, or Max the destroyer might decide to eat it for a snack."

Gabi pretended fear as she snatched her dress and

headed in the opposite direction of the truck and its zealous, large dog, which Annie could see jumping and barking in the bed. He was huge.

"Looks like we have a live one," she said, glad to have something to distract her from the talk of weddings and Colt. She'd had him on her mind constantly. She ushered in the rambunctious giant of a dog and his petite owner, Ginger. Honestly, Annie couldn't figure out why a woman would want a dog that big. Max came bounding into the clinic, towing Ginger as if she was a low-flying kite. He padded with purpose and intent straight behind the counter, placed one big paw on either side of her chair and immediately tried to lick Annie to death.

It took Annie, Gabi, Susan and Ginger to get the affectionate mutt into the exam room. Annie was breathing hard as everyone got into the room and she closed them inside. "Whew, what a job," she muttered, heading to her desk. She'd just sat down when Colt drove into the parking lot. Her stomach flopped over like Max wanting a belly rub. She reminded herself that she was mad at him, and that she was praying for wisdom where he was concerned. Belly flopping was not part of the plan. But watching the handsome bull rider walk through the doors as if he were on a mission and that mission was her...well, it did things to a girl. Even one bent on keeping her distance.

"Okay, look." Colt stopped just on the other side of her desk. "I know you were mad at me last night. And I know you had a right to be, since I went and stepped on your toes about the mutton bustin'. But..." He glanced around as if realizing for the first time that they might not be alone. "Well, you know, since—can we go outside?" he asked.

Annie was already on her way. She flounced past him on her own mission to get him out of the office and on his way as quickly as possible.

Once she broke into the heated day, she spun around. They'd not spoken much on the way home from the rodeo. They hadn't needed to speak, because Leo had rattled on and on excitedly about the mutton bustin' he was going to do. Thanks to Colt opening his mouth and stepping in on her territory.

"You set me up as the bad guy last night," she snapped, suddenly realizing another piece of the puzzle. "You knew all night that riding bulls makes me nervous. You knew that and yet you jumped in there before I could say no, and you okayed mutton bustin'."

"It's just a kid riding a sheep, Annie."

"A sheep today, a bull tomorrow. Don't look at me like that. Isn't that how you got interested?"

He clammed up on that one.

"Well, isn't it?"

"Well, yeah, it was fun when I got the chance to do it. Although I didn't actually get to do it on the up-and-up. I had to sneak into the neighbor's corral and ride when no one was watching."

Annie crossed her arms and glared at him. He stepped close, his eyes searching hers, and her pulse quickened. She fought to keep her defenses sharp and up. Hard to do when Colt's warm molasses eyes made her heart feel like melting butter. He sighed, dropped his head and stared at his boots. He was so close she could feel the drum of his heart on the breath between them. *What, oh what, was going on?*

Colt lifted his gaze, the torture resting in them tearing at Annie's heart just as he stepped in close, wrapped his good arm around her and pulled her to him.

Annie was too shocked to move.

Their faces nose to nose, their lips so close she could feel his tremble, their hearts pounded together and Annie feared that if he let her go her knees would buckle and she'd just sink into a puddle at his feet. To stop that from happening, she grasped his good shoulder and held on.

Though letting go of her was not his plan. Oh no, not a word was spoken as his arm tightened around her and his lips captured hers, stealing her breath and curling her toes, her hair and her heart.

Annie's fingers tightened. She couldn't think. She really couldn't think about anything except how wonderful his kiss was, how utterly... *No!*

Annie forced herself to push out of his arms. He blinked, as if he was just as stunned by what had happened as she was.

He swallowed. She gulped. They stared at each other, both blinking as silence stretched between them.

He rubbed his temple. "Look, Annie, I'm sorry. That shouldn't have happened. I came here to tell you I was sorry. If you don't want Leo to ride, I'll tell him, make some kind of excuse, since it was me who got him all hopped up about it."

Annie pressed her hand to her stomach and willed herself to speak. She could. She remembered when she was able to form coherent words. "Tha—that won't be necessary."

He looked as amazed by her words as she was.

"It won't be necessary?" His brows practically intertwined above his confused eyes.

Annie tried to make herself get over the kiss. It had been a big fat mistake. Sure, there was attraction between them, but with this triangle of a relationship that they now had with each other and Leo, there was no way they could ever complicate it with anything romantic. "You are his daddy and you do have a right to voice your opinion. I would appreciate discussing things before overruling me in the future. However, I do also need to begin to let go. I can't coddle Leo forever. I wanted him to have a male influence in his life, and this is a guy thing."

"Little girls love it, too."

"I should have known. Look, I'd better get back inside. When would be a good time for me to have Leo at your house, or wherever it is that you two will train for this event?"

"I'll have a riding dummy rigged up this afternoon. Come anytime after you get home from work." Colt smiled, turned and sauntered to his truck, whistling. Colt was a whistler...who'd have ever thunk it?

She spun to make her escape back into the clinic. "Annie," he called, halting her steps.

"Yes."

"About that kiss."

Her heart fluttered. "Yes," she said, fighting back the memory of his lips on hers.

"You don't have to worry. It won't be happening again. I promise."

* * *

"I promise." Colt muttered the words a few hours later as he rigged a small barrel between two trees. Ropes suspended the barrel a few inches from the ground, just high enough for Leo's feet not to drag. Tugging the rope tight, he yanked the knot taut. As taut as his frustrations.

They would be here any moment and he was all fumble fingers. He'd tied these knots three times before getting them tight enough. He'd been that way since he'd made a fool of himself by kissing Annie in front of the vet clinic. He'd done it before he could get ahold of his senses. She'd been standing there raking him over the coals, and then he'd kissed her. She was beautiful and...

And he'd been a mess from that moment on.

The memory of the touch of her lips sent an electric thunderstorm moving through him. Stepping back from the barrel, he grabbed the lead rope that would enable him to control the barrel while Leo tried to ride it. Wrapping the hand of his arm with the broken collarbone, he tugged on the rope. The movement sent a small amount of pain through his shoulder, but not much. It wouldn't be long before his arm would be working again. Unlike his brain.

"What were you thinking, Holden?" he muttered again, just as he heard chatter coming through the woods. Leo had arrived. Colt's heart expanded at the sight of his son. Love like he'd never felt threatened to take him to his knees.

Dear God, let me be good enough for this task. The prayer filled him, even though he knew he'd never measure up. Not alone. But with God's help, he'd have to muddle through.

When Annie stepped into view, her silken golden hair glistening, his stomach tightened, his heart suddenly plunged to his boots and his hands dampened. He knew without calling the doctor that he had a major ailment.

Oh yeah, he was sick all right. Sick in the head. What had he been thinking? That she was beautiful, full of fire and coals, and spunk.

"Hey, Colt, I been waitin' all day to see you." Leo raced from the woods and threw his arms around Colt's legs. Colt's heart exploded with love, and it was all he could do not to bend down and hug Leo tight.

But he didn't. A dark emotion hunkered at the back of his joy, the voice telling him he wasn't worthy to take the gift offered to him. Helping Leo, feeling that small thrill of joy at just seeing his smile, felt like much more than he deserved…but he couldn't help himself. And Annie… Colt looked up from his child wrapped around his leg and met her wary gaze.

"Hey," he managed, though his mouth was dry and the words sounded rough. He cleared his throat—and tried to clear his head. This was about Leo. "I've got it all set up."

"What is it?" Leo asked as Annie ran her fingers over the barrel and Leo pushed it.

"You'll sit on there and hold on, while I pull this rope and make it rock. You'll have to hold on and learn to use your legs to help you keep your seat on it."

"Like a sheep," Annie said.

"I get it!" Leo exclaimed and batted saucer-sized eyes at them. "Can I get on now, can I?"

Colt laughed, scooped him up, putting his hands under Leo's arms, and deposited him on top of the barrel. His shoulder protested a little, but not much. "Hold on to that rope I've attached to the barrel."

Leo chattered up a storm as Colt got him situated. Annie stood quietly, her arms crossed, watching from a few feet back. He wondered what she was thinking. Probably that she'd like to wring his neck…or worse.

Theirs was a complicated situation. No denying it.

"Okay, are you hanging on? Got your grip on the rope? That's right, just like that. We're going to have to pick you up a pair of small gloves at Pete's Feed store, but lookin' good right now."

Leo was concentrating too hard to do anything but nod. It was easy to tell the little fella had been watching bull riding and knew the stance coming out of the chute. He had his hand palm up between the barrel and the rope. He had his eyes fixed forward and down, chin dipped, and as Colt stepped back Leo lifted his left arm up over his head. It hit Colt then just how much he did look like a small version of himself. Colt had seen plenty of pictures of himself in that moment and watched hours of film studying his technique to know that Leo wasn't copying just any bull rider. He was copying Colt. Jennifer was responsible for that.

In her own weird way she'd given them a connection, though she'd never revealed the truth to him. For that, at least, he could thank her.

It was a connection Annie wasn't sure about, and wasn't in agreement about. But she was putting her own feelings aside to allow this for him. For that he appreciated her.

"Here we go. Now, practice gripping the barrel with your thighs. That's this part." He placed his hand on

Leo's thigh. "You've got muscles there that you will depend on."

Leo looked up and nodded impatiently. Colt chuckled. "Okay, buddy, get ready to ride." With that he pulled gently on the rope, making the barrel move slightly, just enough to warn Leo how it felt. And then he pulled a little harder.

Leo hooted and yanked his arm and stayed on for a few seconds, and then he slid off into the dirt, which Colt had turned up with a shovel to make soft for just such a situation. Leo laughed, rolled out of the way of the barrel and hopped to his feet.

"That was awesome—let's do it again!"

"Hop on," Colt said, not able to wipe the grin stuck to his face. This was his kid, all right. His son.

"Great ride, Leo." Despite her trepidation, Annie was all smiles.

"I know I did," Leo hollered, busting with admiration and pride. Totally full of himself. Colt thought that was hilarious and would have to give him a little rougher ride so the little fella wouldn't start letting a big ego ruin his determination.

Obviously on the same wavelength, Leo walked over to him all business. "Colt, don't ya know you gotta move this barrel faster if you want me to win. How am I supposed to learn if I don't fall off a few times?"

Colt grimaced and met Annie's watchful stare. "He's got a point. You ready for this?"

Annie bit the inside of her lip and contemplated his words. He figured she was ready to throttle him for the whole situation—kiss included—but she sucked in an extremely deep breath. "I trust you. Do what you think is safe."

Colt couldn't help the smile that lifted one corner of his mouth and traveled across his face in a warm path of admiration. This woman had heart. Colt and Leo weren't the only two in the group with their share of determination.

"Thanks for the vote of confidence. Hop on and hang on, son, because—" His words jerked to a halt. Annie's eyes grew the size of his truck tires. Leo blinked at them.

"I'm hanging on, Colt," he said, unaware of what Colt had said.

Colt calmed his nerves. People used the term *son* all the time. Leo had no clue that for the first time in his life he'd actually heard his daddy call him son.

That struck Colt as the saddest thing. A kid deserved to hear his daddy call him son. A daddy deserved to hear his son call him Dad.

It took every ounce of determination Colt possessed to remind himself that there were some who didn't deserve anything…and he was one of them.

Chapter Twelve

Annie stood on the plank sidewalk of Mule Hollow and stared down the town's Main Street. She loved this town—it was amazing how quickly the place had grown on her. And how could it not with its crazy colors? Why, just seeing the colorful buildings perked up her spirits. And she could sure use some perking up. She felt like a guitar string pulled so tight it quivered with the temptation to snap at any minute. She pushed that out of her mind and focused on the town. There was Heavenly Inspirations Hair Salon, owned by Montana's cousin Lacy Brown Matlock. The two-story building was as pink as a sassy flamingo! Out front was Lacy's 1958 pink convertible Caddy with tail fins and all. Annie had a flash of Elvis hopping from that caddy and looking around the wacky little town and wondering what rabbit hole he'd fallen into.

Pete's Feed and Seed was bright yellow with vibrant green trim. Every building had its own wild combination of colors as if they'd chosen the colors wearing blindfolds.

A smile hovered on Annie's lips as she walked into

the feed store. Joy—that was the color of this town. With its overflowing flower boxes, which were being maintained through the drought by consistent care and watering from some of the residents. Annie knew everyone was praying for rain, but so far the dry, cracked earth had no reason to hope it was getting a drink anytime soon. Miss Adela had said that the Lord had a reason for withholding the rain, and it would come in God's time.

As Annie was standing there, a truck turned onto Main and pulled into the parking space in front of her. It was Colt, of all people.

"And we meet again," he drawled, rubbing his clean-shaven jaw as he got out of his truck.

She couldn't seem to do anything without running into Colt. "Imagine seeing you here," she said. Irritation pricked at the attraction that instantly made itself known to her.

"Fancy finding you here," he said, tugging the brim of his hat lower over his eyes as he studied her. "I figured you'd be working."

"I had to pick up some supplies that Pete ordered for the clinic," she explained. "And I was going to pick up Leo a pair of gloves."

Colt smiled a lazy smile that tickled her insteps. "I came to pick him out a pair myself."

"Oh," she mumbled. "Well, okay. I'll just pick up the supplies. I wouldn't know what he needed anyway."

He nodded toward the store. "Want to pick them out together?"

"I guess." *Not really.*

His eyes crinkled. "I know you're having a hard time with this, but thanks. He's enjoying it. And it's good for him. A kid like him craves the challenge." Colt's gaze skimmed down her jeans-clad body, then stopped momentarily on her lips.

She forced a smile and tried not to think about what lingered between them. She'd had enough on her mind without thinking about the kiss. But despite everything, it hovered on the edge of every thought she had, waiting to set butterflies loose inside her.

"It's all he talks about," she managed as Colt's gaze met hers.

They headed inside the dusty store. Annie figured nothing had changed inside since the day Pete had opened the place.

"Well, hey there," Pete greeted them from behind the counter. Annie had been in once before to pick up some supplies and had met the jovial man already. He was tall and balding, with an easygoing way about him as he tugged a pencil from behind an ear. "Y'all need some help?"

It struck Annie that the feed store owner thought they were together. He'd just assumed it when they'd walked in together.

"I'm picking up the clinic's supplies," she said, trying to clear up his misunderstanding.

"Oh, yeah. I've got it ready." He strode to the side and picked up a large box that had some galvanized metal feed buckets and spray bottles piled inside. Setting it on the counter, he grinned. "It's kinda heavy." He winked. "But Colt can carry it for you."

"That won't be necessary. I can carry it myself."

Pete gave Colt an amused grin. "Have you lost your touch?"

Colt chuckled. "Looks that way."

He didn't seem like a guy loaded down with survivor's guilt or a load of worry. He seemed like any other cowboy teasing about flirting with a girl. But he wasn't any other cowboy—he was Colt Holden, father of her nephew, and he was teasing about flirting with her.

"Do you want to look at those gloves now?" she asked, hearing the irritation in her tone. "I need to get back to work."

"Oh, are you buying Leo some leather gloves for mutton bustin'?" Pete asked.

Did *everyone* in the county know about Leo and his mutton riding?

"Yup," Colt supplied. "He's an excited little rascal. And he's going to enter the roping, too. He's got promise."

Pete crossed his arms over his thick stomach. "Did his daddy like to do this sort of thing?"

The innocent question caught Annie off guard. "Yes, as a matter of fact, he did. Can you show us the gloves, Pete? I really have to go."

"Sure, but Colt knows where they are."

To her relief, Colt led the way to the back wall that was hidden by tall shelves. Spending time with Colt had not been in her plan. Standing in the corner with him certainly hadn't been. She was far too aware of him as a man, and that made not thinking about the kiss impossible in close quarters. She hadn't wanted to admit that it had been a *fantastic* kiss. She'd been trying and trying to avoid that word. But gloomily she admitted that it was a true and uncolored description of the event.

Colt picked a pair of tiny gloves off the rack and held

them out to her. "Hold this one," he said, and looked amused when she made sure their fingers didn't touch when she took them from him.

While she fingered the soft leather glove, he pulled another one from the rack and fingered it, then put it back without offering it to her. At last he found another pair he seemed to like and handed them to her. When she went to take them, he held on and tugged gently, teasing her. She gave him a cool-eyed look. He tugged again and the corners of his mouth quivered. She fought the attraction and tugged harder, glaring at him. He let go and chuckled.

"You aren't in a very good mood today."

"Aren't *you* a master of observation."

He studied her for a long moment, dust motes floating on a sunbeam from a corner window peeking above the shelves.

"You sure do look pretty today, Annie."

Her eyes narrowed. "You don't need to be noticing how I look," she shot back indignantly.

"Maybe not, but it's true. If you'd get that chip off your shoulder, it'd be better."

"If you'd tell your son the truth, it would be better."

"Not going to happen," he said, glancing around to make sure no one else had entered the store. "It's best for everyone if we keep things just like they are."

Annie knew he was right. "True, and it would help if you didn't grab me up and kiss me like you did the other day."

Annie fingered the gloves and tried not to want the cowboy to kiss her. She tried not to want to help him overcome his past. But deep down she wished she was woman enough to do it. But that would mean letting her defenses down. That would mean getting closer to him... risking opening her heart up to him. Could she risk that? Her past held her back. Opening her heart meant trusting Colt with it, and no, she just couldn't do it...could she?

"*Kissing.* Did she say he kissed her?"

"Hush, Esther Mae," Norma Sue grunted, elbowing her sassy friend in the ribs. "She said that and if you hadn't been yakking you'd a heard him say he was Leo's daddy."

Esther Mae's mouth fell open. "We were right!"

Standing in the back room of the feed store, the two ladies were gathering up feed bags to use to decorate a display at Gabi's wedding. They just happened to be standing beside the vent when Annie and Colt's conversation rode through the drafty vent where the old pipe stove used to connect the two rooms years and years ago. The conversation wafted clear as a bell through the vents to the unsuspecting twosome, and they froze in their tracks.

"What are you two up to?" Adela asked, coming around the corner from where she'd been going through a box of supplies that Pete had ordered for them.

Esther Mae waved Adela to silence.

Norma Sue looked worriedly at Adela. "Maybe we should get out of here for a little while."

Adela looked curiously at her just as she heard the voices.

"Annie, come on. I know you're mad at me because I won't tell Leo I'm his daddy. I can't do it, and I...I can't explain it."

"It has to do with the wreck, doesn't it?"

"Yes. It does. Looking at Leo fills me with joy. Hope. Kissing you, Annie, that was like the Fourth of July. I don't know about you, but it blew me out of the stirrups. I don't deserve to feel feelings like that. And you're just the opposite—by the look on your face, you don't want a repeat performance."

Adela's blue eyes were shocked. "We need to go, girls. This is a private conversation."

"I don't want the kiss," Annie said forcibly. "But Leo needs to know you are his daddy. Jennifer was wrong to keep it from you. I don't know if I can sit back and keep up this lie. Not when I think you need Leo as much as he needs you."

"Shoo, girls, now." Adela pushed her frozen-to-the-floor posse members, who were gaping at the vent as if it were a wide-screen television.

"Yeah, you're right," Norma Sue whispered, starting to walk away. She turned back, grabbed Esther Mae by the arm and yanked. "Come on, Miss Snoop!"

Esther Mae stumbled along, stuttering. "Hey, wait— I was, I was *just* making sure we heard right."

"Oh, we heard right," Norma Sue snapped, now that they were out back on the loading dock where there were two rooms between them and the tell-all vent pipe.

Adela was a little pale. "I am really distressed."

"Well, sure we are," Esther Mae gushed. "Why, that poor little boy not knowing his hero is his daddy."

"No," Adela said, her soft voice quivering with shame. "That was a private conversation. It was never meant for us to hear."

"Humph," Norma Sue snorted. "Everything happens

for a reason. And you can't tell me that wasn't one of those times. We weren't standing in that spot by accident."

Esther Mae turned pink with delight. "We certainly weren't. Why, if we hadn't stopped by Lacy's to say hello, we would have been in the front of the feed store when those two came in. And if we hadn't suddenly gotten the inspiration to use feed sacks, we wouldn't have been anywhere near that vent."

"That's right," Norma Sue assured them. "Five minutes and none of that would have come together. Adela, you were the one with the feed sack inspiration. Admit it. You said it was as if the Lord placed the idea in your head it was so perfect."

Adela sighed. "Yes, I said that. However, I'm not an eavesdropper and I don't like it.... Those poor dears. What a dilemma. And that sweet little Leo."

Norma Sue and Esther Mae raised eyebrows at each other over their sweet friend's soft white hair.

"That boy needs a family." Esther Mae wagged her red head. "And Colt needs a reason to keep on going."

Norma Sue's smile was pure mischief. "And they were sure sounding tore up over that kiss. What do you think, Adela? I mean, we can't turn back the clock and undo that we heard it."

Adela batted her brilliant blue eyes. Her friends knew and respected her wisdom in times like these.

"I believe if the Lord truly did put us in that spot by divine appointment, He'll set up the opportunity for us to see His way."

"That's true." Norma Sue thoughtfully considered all that had happened. "We'll know."

Esther Mae let out a long, exaggerated sigh. "But that poor little boy needs—"

Adela touched her friend's arm. "Esther Mae, trust the Lord. Has He ever let you down? Or us?"

"Well, no. But, you know I'm impatient."

Norma Sue stuffed her hands in her coverall pockets and rocked back on her boots. "Hang on for God's time, Esther Mae. You know good and well that's the best time there is."

"Okay," Esther Mae huffed, "I'll tap my toe and wait. You two just remember that I don't like it, not one little bit."

Norma Sue shook her head. "Do you think me and Adela will have one moment's peace with you reminding us every day over and over again just how much you are not happy with the situation, that we will have a chance of not rememberin' that you don't like waiting? I can only wish!"

"Ladies," Adela interrupted. "Your exuberance for the plan the Lord has set up for us is commendable. I do believe this calls for a cup of coffee and some of my Sam's coconut pie."

"And I do believe you are right. Don't you agree, Esther Mae?"

Esther Mae started walking fast down the sidewalk, her hips swinging double time. "Let's go, girls," she called over her shoulder. "I've been dieting far too long. It's time for a reward. Look out, Sam, here we come." Walking even faster, she added, "And maybe we can talk up a plan. It never hurts to be prepared. We're the posse, after all."

Norma Sue hooted and Adela chuckled.

* * *

Annie sat in the patio chair that Colt had borrowed from Montana and Luke. He'd said if she was going to be spending her evenings having to watch him and Leo toss a rope that she needed to be comfortable. It was a nice gesture, and she'd been very comfortable all week long as she sat and watched Leo and Colt work tirelessly on the barrel riding and the steer dummy roping.

Annie prayed more and more that God would work out the situation between Leo and Colt. Her and Colt's situation, however, she continued to hold off. But it was a lie to think that there wasn't a connection radiating between them. It scared her. And she thought it scared him, too. Or he didn't think he deserved to feel a connection like that. She'd begun to suspect that more and more every day. Sitting in the chair, observing them, gave a person some time to think. She was certain Colt loved and adored Leo.

Gabi had arranged it so that Colt was going to bring them to the wedding. She'd said that even if Colt wasn't going to admit to the public that Leo was his, he was going to bring him to the wedding, and the photographer was going to get plenty of shots of them together. She'd been told the story of how Leo adored Colt, and Gabi wanted to document the fact.

Annie had no way of saying no to that, and so she would be escorted to Gabi and Jess's wedding by Colt. It was a nerve-racking thought.

The plan had been revealed to her today and her stomach was still rolling.

"Aunt Annie," Leo called, shocking Annie by putting the *aunt* first…but then it really wasn't a shock.

Leo was growing up. She'd seen something else in him change since they'd been hanging around with Colt. He seemed more secure. More confident. The Annie Aunt tag was her special nickname, but Annie knew with maturity things would change. It was a normal, good thing.

"What, kiddo?"

"I'm working my spurs," he called, and as Colt pulled the rope, Leo pulled his knees up, then let his heels come down on the sides of the barrel as if he were riding a bull. To her dismay, he had great form.

"Pull me faster, Colt!" he called, doing well as the barrel went back and forth.

Smiling, Colt yanked a little harder. "Ride 'em, cowboy," he called, and gave it another gentle yank.

"Yee-haw!" Leo yelled just before he lost his balance and fell into the soft dirt. He yelled in pain the moment he hit the dirt—Colt and Annie reacted instantly.

Colt was closer and was kneeling beside him first.

"What's wrong, son?" he asked, worry etching his face.

Leo was writhing and holding his shoulder. Colt cringed.

"My arm," Leo whimpered.

"Looks like we need to make a trip to the Ranger emergency room."

"Ohhh," Annie groaned. "He could have a break."

Gathering him up, Colt used his healthy arm to carry Leo to the car. Annie followed him as he strode to his truck. "Do you want to drive and me to hold him, or do you want to hold him and me to drive?"

"My hands are shaking. Do you think you could drive?"

"Hop in. Let's roll." After she climbed into the seat and got strapped in, he gently placed Leo in her arms.

"It's going to be okay," he said, then hurried around and slid behind the wheel.

Within minutes they were on the road and heading to Ranger. It was an hour drive to Ranger. Leo groaned as they hit a bump.

The look of alarm on Colt's face as he looked in their direction made Annie's heart jerk even harder. The love mixed with terror for his son was unmistakable. Annie held Leo loosely so she wouldn't hurt him more and prayed that God would get them safely to the emergency room.

Chapter Thirteen

"Thanks, Doctor," Colt said, shaking the doctor's hand.

Annie hugged Leo and shook the young doctor's hand, too. "We appreciate all you've done."

The doctor grinned. "It's what I do. Take care, Leo. And better luck on the next rodeo."

Leo looked a little forlorn. "I sure wanted to ride in that rodeo." He held his arm up with its brand-new, bright blue cast. "But I got this now."

"And all your friends can sign it," Annie reminded him.

"Oh, yeah." He grinned up at Colt. "Can you give me your autograph?"

Colt looked torn, confusing Annie yet again. He'd probably signed many, many autographs. Was he conflicted because Leo was his son? That didn't strike her as the reason he was acting weird.

"You know, Leo, maybe you should just have your friends sign your cast."

Leo frowned. "But I want you. You're my hero."

Colt pulled a pen out of his pocket. "I'll sign, but I'm just a cowboy, Leo. I happen to be good at riding bulls.

Heroes are people who make a difference in people's lives. I want you to know that. I'm signing this because you're my…my friend. Okay?"

Leo grinned. "I like being your friend. But you *are* a hero. You just don't know it."

Annie's heart warmed at Leo's words. He was encouraging Colt. Colt was inspiring kids to achieve success and he was doing it by being a good role model. In that, he was a hero.

She'd been so worried about Leo, it had been a relief to have Colt with them.

As it was. He helped Leo off the examining table and, with a grin her way, they all walked out the door and down the hall. Nurses who had helped them waved and called goodbye. A few recognized Colt, and she could tell they had gotten special attention from a couple of them that had nothing to do with the fact that Leo was a darling little boy with a broken arm. Colt hadn't flirted back when they'd flirted and, in fact, he'd looked uncomfortable even.

"Tell the nice ladies goodbye, Leo. And thank them for fixing you up real nice," Colt said, placing a possessive hand on Leo's shoulder.

"Yes, sir," Leo said. "Y'all did real good," he called. "Thanks."

"Watch out for the barrels and the ground next time," one of the younger nurse's aides said as she came around the desk and smiled at Leo. Annie didn't miss that she touched Colt's arm and slid a folded paper into his hand. Annie almost gasped out loud, she was so shocked by the woman's actions. But it was the jealousy that curled in the pit of her stomach that shocked her the most. They weren't a couple, but this nurse didn't know that, yet she was stuffing her phone number into his palm.

As they exited the building, she was feeling really low. She faced the fact that she'd been thrilled and relieved that Colt was with her during the emergency. He'd taken control and made her feel that everything was going to be okay. His support had…it had touched her. That feeling had dissipated the instant he'd accepted the note.

As they were passing a trash can beside the exit door, she was startled once more when he quietly dropped the note inside. Annie's heart soon strummed with happiness. Colt caught her looking and winked.

A warm smile spread across her face and there was absolutely no way she could stop it from happening.

Leo fell asleep in the truck almost before they'd left the parking lot. Annie glanced into the backseat where he'd leaned his head against the armrest. "He's out," she said as she faced back toward the road. "This wore him down."

"It's made for a late night. Did you realize it's almost midnight?"

Annie propped her elbow on the door and rubbed her forehead with her fingertips. "No wonder Leo's passed out."

"He was a little trouper, wasn't he?" Colt looked proud and it did something to her insides. Almost everything he did or said, every look he gave her, caused her to feel something.

"Thank you for being there," she said, sitting up straight and facing him as best she could. She couldn't chance saying he was his daddy, not even with Leo sleeping. What if he overheard her? No, she didn't want to take that risk.

"Hey, I'm glad I was. I feel bad." He briefly met her eyes in the dim light of the dashboard. "You can say I told you so if you want."

She chuckled. "I'm not saying that. I'm sorry he got hurt, but I guess if you're going to be good at something you're going to have ups and downs as you hone your skills. Leo was really enjoying himself."

"So was I. Annie, thank you for bringing Leo to Mule Hollow to meet me. I need to tell you that." She didn't look at him but saw his good hand grip the wheel tighter.

She sighed. "That's why I came. When I got trapped in the shed and couldn't get out and I thought I was going to die...all I could think about was that Leo was going to have to go into foster care because he had no one. Or at least they believed he had no one." Tears welled in her eyes, and when she looked at Colt there was no way to hide them. "He deserved better than that. I've told you all of this before. But, well, it was a relief to me tonight to have you there."

They stared at each other for a heartbeat before he looked back at the road. Annie found herself wishing... she pushed the thought out of her crazy head. She wasn't wishing for anything except for Colt to admit to Leo that he was his daddy. She closed her eyes in the darkness and prayed that it would be so. That Colt would deal with whatever was keeping him from admitting it.

And she tried her best not to think about how much his presence, his kiss and his strength meant to her as a woman. This was all about Leo.

"I still can't believe," Colt said, looking at Leo in the

rearview mirror. No mistaking, the kid was sacked out sound asleep. His eyes were closed and he snored gently against the armrest. "I can't believe I missed out on this little guy. I mean, I know my career was my life and I made that clear to women who were interested. I just didn't want any of them to get the idea that I was anywhere near settling down. I had no intention of stringing anyone along." He concentrated on the driving, watching the road intently. "I have enough memories of a childhood gone bad to last me a lifetime. I certainly didn't want to string anyone along."

"Can I ask about your childhood?" Annie asked.

Colt told her about his alcoholic dad and the neglect. He told her about his mother leaving and how Luke had taken responsibility for him and Jess. "When we moved here, I think my dad was running from bill collectors. Luke found a real job here working for Clint Matlock's dad, Mac. Our life started getting better then, because Luke was such a mature kid and took on a lot. And the town was good to us. Mac would pay Luke bonuses for working hard. It was his way of helping without making us think we were taking charity. Of course, I was too young and Luke always made sure I had food."

He didn't talk about his past to anyone but Jess and Luke. And even then not much. His mother was back in their lives, but it hadn't been easy. They'd all made their peace with her, because as Luke said, it was the right thing to do. But she wasn't in the picture much, since she lived in Fredericksburg. He told this to Annie, too.

Annie ran her long, slender finger along the edge of the console, Colt liking the look of her hands. He liked the look of Annie. She was thin, but not as thin as when she'd first come to town.

"You were lucky to have Luke and Jess," she said. "You were only two years older than Leo when your parents basically abandoned you."

"You were younger than that, weren't you?" he observed. "How could anyone leave their kids on a church step and walk away? Especially a two-year-old and a three-year-old?"

"We had messed-up childhoods, Colt. But I don't want that for Leo. I'm so glad I brought him here."

When they finally reached Annie's house, Leo woke as Colt carried him inside. Annie wasn't sure how Colt managed it with his injured arm, but he insisted on carrying his son. Annie watched Colt place Leo in his bed after she'd turned back his covers. Her heart ached for the tender picture they made. "You did good, little buddy," Colt told him quietly, his voice husky.

Leo looked half-asleep. "You did, too." He sighed, his eyes closed as he drifted back off. "I love you…." His words slurred as he curled up and was gone.

Colt froze. Annie's heart clutched tightly for Leo. When Colt looked up at her from where he knelt, smoothing his son's forehead, there was no denying the moisture glistening in his eyes.

"This is special, isn't it?"

Annie wrapped her arms tight across her stomach and tried to lock her heart down, but it was impossible. "There's nothing like it," she whispered, knowing the undeniable truth—Colt Holden did something to her that breached her defenses and tempted her to let them fall away completely.

Colt looking at his son with such love filled her with longing for the family she'd always dreamed of. The family she was too afraid to open her heart to.

Colt followed Annie out onto the porch. His heart was full and every fiber in him wanted to claim Leo as his. It was a burning desire that seared his soul and cried out for the missing portion. On the porch he grabbed Annie in a tight hug. She was startled. "Thank you, Annie. Thank you for bringing my son into my life."

She was speechless and he could understand why, since he'd grabbed her roughly, like a madman. Letting her go, he strode toward his truck. He needed to put distance between them and the feeling of home and hearth that had settled around him like the wrappings of a long-dreamed-of Christmas present. This was a present he didn't deserve, and he couldn't let himself linger too long in the land of fantasy.

Distance and the light of day. That's what he needed. Tomorrow he'd have his head on straight. Tomorrow he'd have his heart put back behind the shield he'd come to need where Leo—and Annie—were concerned.

Chapter Fourteen

"Aunt Annie," Leo said the next morning. His hair was tousled from sleep as he scooted into the chair and stared at the cocoa cereal she'd poured into his bowl.

"Yes, sweetie. You feeling all right this morning?" Annie had checked him through the night. Not sleeping much herself, she'd been pleased to see that his slumber had been deep.

"Yes, ma'am." He studied his cereal and then looked thoughtfully up at her. "I wish Colt was my daddy."

And there it was. Air whooshed out of Annie as if she'd been punched in the stomach. What could she say to that? She had been totally naive to not think this was coming.

"Well, he signed your cast. That's special, isn't it? Eat up, honey, we're running late today."

She couldn't look at her nephew. Couldn't tell him what she knew in her heart was the right thing to say… and it broke her heart. The memory of Colt's arms holding her close sent butterflies swarming across her heart.

Shaken, she hurried to dress for work and didn't let her thoughts dwell on the emotions swirling around her about Colt. This was about Leo. It had always been about Leo.

And Leo wanted his daddy.

Could she change this for the little boy she loved more than anything in the world?

Pausing while putting on her mascara, Annie met her own gaze in the mirror. "You are going to give Leo his daddy." She hiked a brow. "And you aren't going to stop until it is a reality. No backing down." Nodding at her reflection, she caught the glint of determination in her eyes. It dug deep. "No backing down," she repeated with a determination that refused to be denied.

Gabi and Montana were thrilled to have Annie drop Leo off at their house after work that afternoon. The two secret aunts were about to burst, wanting to spoil Leo. The desire for Leo to have it all was pushing Annie on as she hugged Gabi.

"Wish me luck... I mean, pray for me."

"We've got your back, Annie. Jess and Luke are right here with us. Leo is a pure gift from God. And you don't know it yet, but so are you. If you hadn't come, this wouldn't be a possibility. In the midst of his pain and his tragedy, God's had a plan."

"Colt has to agree to it, though," Annie reminded her.

Montana came back from getting Leo set up with cookies at the kitchen table. "We're going to pray for his heart and his eyes to be opened. Now, you go get him, Annie."

Colt tested his shoulder as he tugged a bale of hay from the back of the flatbed trailer. The sun was a sizzler today. He felt certain that if he laid a piece of bacon on the steel wheel guard of the trailer, it would fry within minutes.

In the distance there was a dark cloud forming. It was the first hint of rain in months. Studying the cloud, Colt paused to swipe his forehead with the back of his arm, and he prayed that God would see fit to bless Mule Hollow with a good, soaking rain. And then he went back to unloading the hay. Heat or rain, it felt good to be exerting his pent-up energy.

Especially when his thoughts were so jumbled up. He hadn't slept at all after dropping Annie and Leo off at home. He hadn't wanted to leave. It had been all he could do to walk out of the house and leave them behind.

Part of the reason he'd been so disturbed was that it wasn't only Leo he didn't want to leave, but Annie, too.

She'd been so strong during the crisis when Leo had fallen off the barrel. She'd been shaken, yet held it together as they'd loaded him up and headed to the hospital. Colt was angry with God about the unjust death of the Everson family, but he had to be thankful and he had to praise God for sending Annie to keep his child safe and happy during the years when Jennifer had left him out of the equation.

His anger about that still ran high and always would... But Annie had been stuck between a rock and a hard place. He'd forgiven her for that, his resentment having dissipated over time as he watched her with his son.

He thought of how fiercely he'd wanted to hold her when he knew she was worried and trying to be strong. How much he'd wanted to be there for her when she'd told him how much his presence had meant to her.

Colt tossed the hay bale off the truck, then stared off in the distance—he had no right to want more from her. He had no right to want them.

But he did.

A plume of dust rose up over the hill line where the road trailed back in the direction he had come. A car or truck was heading his way. Through his dark aviator shades he watched the car top the hill—Annie.

His insides clamored at the sight of her old car. Stripping off his leather gloves, he hopped from the back of the trailer, his shoulder jarring only a little from the impact.

He tossed his gloves to the trailer and was waiting when she came to a halt. "Hey," he said the minute she got out of the car. "Everything okay? Is Leo all right this morning?"

Annie's brow was knit tight and her eyes were steady on him as she closed her car door. "Leo is good. He's with Montana and Gabi."

"Really." He could see she had something on her mind by the telling sign of her eyes, dulled by sleeplessness or worry.

"They are his aunts." Her eyes flashed. "What are you doing with these bales?" she asked, climbing up on the trailer and staring at the hay bales.

Perplexed by her behavior, Colt decided the smart thing to do in the face of the steam edging from beneath her tightly wound temper was to go with the flow. Let her ease back some of the anger building under there, and then push.

"I'm tossing it off in sections." Before he got the sentence out, she started trying to pick up the bale to throw it off the trailer. Startled by her assertiveness, he could only watch her stubborn attempt at tossing the heavy bale. Grunting, her face was red with exertion and determination. She managed to get the hay bale up, half tossed it with one more push, then got it off the trailer. The woman had something on her mind and it didn't take a genius to figure out what it was. He knew she wanted him to tell Leo he was his daddy.

"You've got muscles for a skinny girl," he teased, because he didn't know what else to say to her. He couldn't tell her what she wanted him to tell her. No matter how much he wanted to.

She was breathing hard from her efforts and glared down at him. "I need to start working out. This is labor intensive."

He chuckled despite the undercurrent running between them. She knew he knew why she was here. Staring at each other, it almost felt as though they were in a boxing ring together and were circling, getting ready to make the next move. "Ranching isn't just watching the grass grow and the cattle eat."

"Ha! Especially right now, when there isn't any grass to speak of." She grunted, taking another deep breath as she eyed another bale.

She was cute, standing up there in her oversize orange T-shirt, jeans and jogging shoes. Her hair was loose today, falling in a silky sheet of gold-and-bronze tones. Looking at her, Colt smiled. It reached in deep, shooting at the darkness curled up inside him.

She reached for another bale, but Colt stopped her. "I need to move the truck down a little ways before dropping more."

She stopped what she was doing and sank to the edge of the trailer, dangling her legs off the side. Instead of hopping to the ground, she remained seated. "Thank you again for being there yesterday."

"I was the cause of his fall. I'm glad I was there to get him some help. I'm going to be there from here on out, Annie. It's going to be all right."

"It's *not* going to be all right, Colt. It's not."

Her words were edged with despair and it tore at Colt, even as he was prepared to deflect her argument that he needed to tell Leo.

"Leo told me this morning, before I took him to day care, that he wished you were his daddy."

Her words were soft-spoken though he knew she wanted to scream them at him. His heart cracked—the pain, a violent quake, rocked through him. Leo wished he was Colt's son.

Every ounce of willpower he had, every bit of strength and skill it took to ride the meanest, toughest bulls he'd ever ridden didn't rank close to what it took to pull the edges of his heart together and force himself to shut down the need to tell Leo the truth. He couldn't do it. Wouldn't.

Colt's disgust with himself was too deep.

"Doesn't that get to you?" she asked.

"Yes, it does. How could it not?"

"Then tell him."

"I can't, Annie. No matter how much I want to do this... Look, Annie, I just can't."

Annie hopped from the trailer and looked up at him, searching his eyes as if she could probe deep enough to find answers.

"Why? Don't you get it, Colt—this morning I couldn't say anything. What was I supposed to say? You'll just have to do with him being your hero, honey, because he's not your dad. *That* would have been a lie. There will be more and more times when I'll be compromised like that. You have to tell him, Colt."

"I don't *have* to do anything, Annie," he said vehemently.

Annie tried to hold on to her temper. It was an odd combination that she felt toward Colt. She wanted to hold him and tell him everything was going to be fine. She wanted to shake him and tell him to step out of the fog of self-pity—but she knew that wasn't what he felt. It was a worthlessness that he felt. But Leo needed him, and with every day that passed she realized more and more how much.

"Colt, I understand that this tragedy that you've lived through has caused you terrible pain and guilt. But you can't continue to use it as an excuse not to claim your child." *Please, Father, help get this through his thick skull!* The prayer shook her. She wanted this more than anything she'd ever wanted. She wanted Colt to be Leo's daddy more than any prayer she'd ever prayed for her parents to come back and claim her as a child. The truth hit her. "Do you know how badly I wanted my parents to walk back into my life and claim me? I prayed every night for that to happen. I'm fairly certain that Jennifer's behavior stems back to our abandonment, too, in its own way. I'm so, so sorry you were hurt by not being told about Leo. I'm so sorry you were hurt by the part you played in the Everson family's deaths. The loss of that sweet family is tragic. But you couldn't help it. And you can't fix it now. The tragedy of you not claiming your son is something you *can* fix. You have control over that. How much more tragic will it be if one day Leo finds out you are his father, and knew it but still didn't claim him?"

Colt strode away from her and she followed him. "Colt, where are you going?"

He spun. "Nowhere. I'm just thinking. Annie, I don't…deserve him."

"Stop that. Stop it right now. God gave him to you, so He must have decided you do deserve him. Jesus died on the cross for us and we don't deserve that, but we got it anyway. Leo was born from you and Jennifer. He's yours. God loves you, Colt Holden, and He knows you're hurting and full of sorrow. And He knows you're angry." Annie pulled the paper that she'd written at work from her pocket. "Colt, Ecclesiastes says, *'There's a time for everything, a time to weep and a time to laugh, a time to mourn and a time to dance.'* There is a time to weep as you're soul has been doing. But now it's time to laugh—and not feel guilty. It's time for you to stop hating yourself for the accident and start loving your son and the life God is giving you the opportunity to have. Your son needs you. Please, please, don't throw away your God-given time with Leo. Don't look back with regret one day." She reached for his hand and placed the paper in his palm, then closed his fingers around the carefully printed words. "Think about it. Pray about it."

Colt stared at the paper in his hand. "I'm not telling Leo."

"Just like that. You've made your choice." There just

was no reasoning with this man! Throwing up her hands, she stomped back toward her car.

She couldn't believe what she was hearing.

"Annie—"

"What?" she asked, whirling around. Her mind was reeling. "I need to get out of here because my mind is stuck on verse three of Ecclesiastes 30."

He blinked. "What does it say?"

"There's a time to kill! That's what it says."

"It also says a time to heal."

"And a time to die."

He shook his head. "Annie, come on. Cut me some slack here."

Annie reached and cupped his face. "Colt, please, *please* wake up. Your son needs you as his daddy. Not as his bull-riding hero. I'll give you time because I have no choice." Before she dropped her hands from his face, she leaned in and kissed him. Her lips met his and the energy surging between them ignited. Annie gasped when Colt's arms came fiercely about her and he pulled her hard against him. Her mind got fuzzy as the sensations overtook all thought. Suddenly he broke the kiss and buried his face in her neck as he clung to her. They were both breathing hard, and Annie couldn't speak, so stunned by what had just passed between them that she couldn't form words. All she could do was know that when he let her go, nothing was ever going to be the same again. Colt Holden had just tipped her world on edge and she was dangerously teetering on falling over.

A time to love... Another line from Ecclesiastes struck her like an arrow to the heart. A time for everything... and this was her time to leave. Pulling out of his arms, they stared at each other, and he looked as stunned as she felt. His warm brown eyes were as muddled as stirred-up muddy water. Annie spun around and this time made it to her car without him following her or calling her back.

It was just as well, because she wouldn't have stopped or turned around this time. She was hightailing it out of Dodge and she was moving fast.

Why, oh why, did love always end up becoming a no-win situation?

Chapter Fifteen

"What do y'all think?" Norma Sue asked as she dis-
played the centerpieces for the tables. They'd taken cans
and wrapped them in pieces of feed sack, then tied colorful ribbons around them. It sounded not so cute, but
the effect was charming and country. Especially when
balanced with the Western-themed lace and rope that
ran down the length of the white tablecloths.

"It's adorable," Gabi assured Norma Sue and the other
ladies waiting for her approval, when Annie, Montana
and Gabi walked into Norma Sue's barn.

Annie had been too upset to say much when she made
it back to the house to pick up Leo. All it had taken was
one look at her face for Montana and Gabi to know
things had not gone well. They'd insisted that she go
with them to help decorate for the wedding reception.
Leo was busy, out in the barn with Luke, bottle-feeding
calves—not that he was doing much more than watching with his arm in a cast. But he was having a blast and
had informed her that when they got through feeding
the calves, he was going to get to muck out some stalls.

"Oh, you are, are you?" she'd said, her heart just

bursting from the joy on his face and the fact that unbeknownst to him he was spending time with his uncle.

"Oh yeah, and it's gonna be fun," he'd said, shaking his head and looking at her with big eyes, as if he knew a secret she didn't know.

Needing the time to chill, Annie had gladly let him stay. She'd needed the time to vent, too. Montana and Gabi were in disbelief, as she was.

"He doesn't think he's worthy," Gabi had assured them. "I'm telling y'all, the cowboy is punishing himself for the deaths of the Eversons, God rest their souls. I don't think anything is going to prove to him any differently."

"Time," Montana said, looking confident as she'd driven them toward town. "Time will heal all wounds… if cared for. We just need to make sure his wound continues to get the balm of love and care applied to it so his heart doesn't scale over with scar tissue."

Annie thought hard about that. Still was, as she looked around the barn at the pretty decorations. This made her heart lighten with joy for Gabi.

"Oh, this is going to be so beautiful." She hugged Gabi. Both she and Montana had taken her in, and in her heart of hearts she thanked God for bringing her here to the family she'd always longed for. She might not be their real relation, but in her heart she could dream. They felt like family, and for Leo they always would be, even if his father never chose to give him his name.

"I love the grapevine and lace," Gabi said, fingering some that lay on the table and being assembled by several smiling ladies, some of whom Annie had met at church. The excitement was rampant in the room and, despite her low mood, she could not help but feel better.

"I'm in awe." Montana laughed, looking around with big eyes. "You ladies amaze me. After all the weddings this town has thrown, it's still like a party up in here!"

Annie laughed with everyone else. Country music was blaring on the radio, and several ladies were boot scootin' across the room in time to the music as they carried various decorations to their destinations. Refreshments were set out on a table and it was literally a free-for-all on helping out.

Looking around at the wedding preparations, Annie's heart swelled up with longing like the many helium balloons Esther Mae was busy filling at a nearby table.

"You need one of these," Esther Mae popped off, smiling as if she'd just read Annie's mind. And she had!

"Come here and help me," the redhead continued, waving her over. Montana and Gabi both got called to duty helping Norma Sue unravel grapevine. So Annie headed to the balloons. Esther Mae handed her one. "Tie these for me while I blow them up. My fingers are cramping, and we need to talk, too."

"That's not the only thing cramping about you," Norma Sue teased. "Her brain's been cramping, too."

"My brain is *not* cramping," Esther Mae huffed.

"Oh, so if that's not the problem, then what is?" Norma Sue hooted.

"The woman should have been a comedian. Just because I was trying to air these up for the longest time with the gas turned off."

"It wouldn't have been so bad except she kept thinking it was bad balloons." Norma Sue winked at Annie and Esther Mae blushed.

"It's true. But hey, if I can't laugh at myself, then what am I going to do?"

"Wonder what everyone else is laughing at." Norma Sue chuckled.

"I know where you live, Norma Sue, and don't you forget it."

"So, we heard you were coming to the wedding with Colt." Esther Mae batted her green eyes at Annie. They were deep in the middle of some mischief making.

"Well, it had been talked about. But I'm not sure."

"Yes, she is," Gabi said, her stubborn chin set as she hiked a brow in challenge. "I'm making sure of it, so you gals don't have to start figuring out a way to make it happen. Colt has his instructions straight from the bride's mouth. And he doesn't want to upset his almost new sis-in-law."

That got some hoots and some claps from everyone. Annie had to chuckle despite the fact that she wasn't too keen on being escorted to the church by Colt. She would do it for Leo. The memory of the kiss heated her cheeks. Everyone instantly thought it was their teasing. They had no idea.

"Well, Gabi if you do all the fix'n up, then what are we all supposed to do? Kinda takes the fun out of it," Norma Sue said.

"Ahem," Annie cleared her throat. "I'm standing right here and no one asked me anything about being fixed up. I'm going to the wedding with Colt because Leo wants to go with Colt."

Norma Sue and Esther Mae looked shamelessly at each other and smiled.

Adela, who was sitting at the end of the table sewing lace to the edge of feed sacks, smiled kindly at her. "Colt and Leo do get along so wonderfully. What a blessing to both of them."

Annie got the weirdest feeling that they knew. "Yes, ma'am, it has been a blessing."

"I personally think Colt needs a good kiss to brighten his days. Annie, what do you think about that?" Esther Mae held out a balloon to her. Instead of the huge smile Annie would have expected, she was very serious. Too serious.

Annie laughed, she was so surprised by her bluntness. "I think if you want to give him a kiss, Esther Mae, he would really appreciate it. More power to you."

That got a hoot from Norma Sue. "Hold on there, let me call him up and warn him."

"Funny, you two. My Hank gets all my kisses, thank you very much. And you know good and well I'm teasing you, Annie, but I know you've thought about it."

"How do you know—" Annie blurted out before she caught herself. They were just probing. They really didn't have any idea that she'd kissed Colt or that she thought about it. How could they? Teasing. That was all they were doing. She was just so stinkin' self-conscious that she'd very nearly given away her secret. And that just would not do. Not at all.

But mad at the man or not, just the thought of that kiss and the way it had shaken her world made her head fuzzy and her pulse start skipping beats as if it were sending out an SOS.

"Know what?" Esther Mae asked, grinning. "Are you saying you *do* want to kiss Colt? Or that maybe you already have. Y'all sure have been spending a lot of time out there at his cabin teaching Leo how to rope and ride."

Annie's mouth fell open. "I thought y'all were sneaky about trying to fix folks up."

"Sneaky." Norma Sue chortled. "When we see a gal and a cowboy we think will match up like the two pieces of a heart locket, we don't have a reason to be sneaky. We give fair warning most times."

"*Most* times," Gabi said. "But I'm sure there are several in this room who got blindsided by the posse and were well on their way to being hitched before they knew what hit them."

From around the room hoots of laughter and agreement erupted along with several folks agreeing they'd been in that position. Annie's stomach hurt.

She was in trouble and she knew it.

She'd fallen in love with the father of her nephew. And if he didn't want Leo, he certainly wouldn't want her.

The matchmaking posse of Mule Hollow had no idea what they were undertaking in this little matchup. But Annie did and she knew it was a long shot. Especially since she knew Colt was ready to run in the opposite way.

The scariest, trickiest part was there sat little Leo smack in the middle of this train wreck.

Trouble? Oh yeah, she was in trouble, no doubt about it. And here she was—the one who didn't like bull riding. She felt as though she'd just hopped in the chute onto the back of the wiliest bull around, the gate was opening and her hand was stuck in the bull rope even before the ride began!

Colt needed to talk to someone, and who better to talk to than his big brother? Pulling into the ranch's drive, he cut the engine and was walking toward the house when he heard a squeal of laughter coming from the barn. Leo.

He hadn't expected that. And he wasn't prepared to see his son right now. Not after what Annie had told him.

"Colt!" Leo came running out of the barn with two milk bottles clutched in his arms.

"Hey, it's easy to see what you've been doing." Colt grinned down at his son, the need to hug him close stronger. It was as if the day before, when he'd gotten to hug Leo and comfort him when he'd been hurt, made him want to feel his child in his arms even more. Six years of hugs he'd missed. It weighed heavily on him as he stooped down. Leo grinned at him and poked a bottle toward him.

"You want some?" He made a face. "It's gross."

"How do you know? I bet the calves aren't grumbling."

"They sure aren't—they loved it! Luke said he thinks God got them mixed up and put little pigs inside them cow hides."

"I sure do," Luke said, coming out of the barn. "You saw it, Leo. You know what I'm talkin' about."

Leo made a disgusted face that would have made anyone laugh. "I never saw so much slobber in all my life."

"They didn't try to kiss you, did they?"

"Try to kiss me? They 'bout licked me to death."

"You do look kind of damp." Colt tugged at Leo's

half-tucked-in shirt, which was damp. "What happened here?"

"That little piglet-calf tried to eat my shirt!"

"I see you lived. And so did your cast."

"It sure did. Look, Luke signed it, too."

Luke was watching him with thought-filled eyes. Colt wondered what his brother was thinking. Luke wanted more than anything for him and Jess to be happy and settled. Colt figured Luke was thinking he was messing up.

"Y'all had an exciting evening yesterday."

"Just a little. Leo slipped off the barrel at just the right angle. He didn't hit abnormally hard or anything."

"It was just one of those things," Leo offered, grinning between them.

Colt gave him a hug. "Yes, it was, but I sure wish it hadn't happened to you, little buckaroo."

"It's okay, Colt. I'll have a whole year to work on my skills now."

His positive attitude was inspiring. "Yes, you will."

"You're gonna still work with me, aren't you, Colt?"

"Sure I am."

"All right!" He started off toward the house. "I gotta take these to the kitchen for Montana when she gets home."

In silence they watched him make his way toward the house. As soon as there was a good distance between them and he wouldn't hear anything, Luke looped his thumbs in his pockets and studied Colt. "That kid is great."

Colt's heart clenched tight. "Yeah, he is."

"What's going on, Colt? I got here and Annie was about as white as a sheet. Montana and Gabi talked her into going to decorate with them hoping to help her feel better."

Colt felt as if he'd been bucked off and slammed into the packed dirt. He didn't like knowing that Annie was still shook up by the time she'd reached the ranch house. But then again, that kiss had shaken him up, too. When she'd taken his face into her hands so unexpectedly, right in the heat of their argument, the tenderness of it had yanked something hard inside him. He'd been wound so tight that her actions, the mere contact of her touch, had buckled him. He'd wrapped his arms around her with a reflex he had no control over, and the touch of her lips to his had reached deep into his soul. The thought of it shook him even now.

He looked down, afraid Luke would see his feelings in his eyes. He wasn't ready to deal with what he felt for Annie at the moment. He had to deal with his emotions about Leo. If he didn't eventually come around to Annie's way of thinking, then the kiss they'd shared didn't matter. The gulf that spanned between them would simply grow too wide to cross.

"Colt," Luke prodded when he didn't answer.

"She told me that Leo told her he wished I was his daddy."

"You *are* his daddy."

"She's furious because I won't tell him. She tried to talk to me about the wreck."

"I can't begin to understand what's happening in your head where the wreck is concerned. The emotions I'm sure are tough in this situation, but Colt, I'm telling you it's time to move forward. If you can't, maybe you need to go see that doctor."

"I don't need the doctor."

Leo came walking from the house with his arms full. On closer inspection, they realized he had three glasses of milk clutched close to him, between his cast and his body. He was grinning.

"I brought us some snacks." Milk sloshed from the glass onto his shirt and his cast. Both Colt and Luke dashed the few feet between them and helped relieve him of his burdens.

"Well, thank you," Luke said, holding his half-full glass up in a salute.

Colt did the same. "I needed this."

"Oh, I got more." Leo reached down into his abnormally shaped shirt that was tucked tightly into his jeans. He tugged and pulled out a plastic bag of cookies. "See." He beamed. "We're gonna make it."

"You know, kid," Luke said, shooting Colt a you-need-to-fix-this look, "you're one smart cookie."

Leo set his glass on the ground, careful not to spill any more than he'd already spilled. He dug into the bag and pulled out a crumbling cookie. "I am. My momma used to tell me all the time it's 'cause I got my daddy's jeans. I don't know what that means, 'cause I'm wearing my own jeans."

Luke chuckled and accepted the cookie Leo passed him. Not done, Leo looked at him as he handed another cookie over. "I told Aunt Annie I wished you were my daddy, Colt."

As if heaping coals on already flaring fire, Montana's truck turned onto the drive and headed toward the house. Colt had spotted Annie's car sitting on the other side of Gabi's truck, hidden from his view when he'd first driven up.

Annie climbed from the truck with Gabi and Montana. She was all smiles as she headed toward them. Colt had dodged a bullet where Leo was concerned. Though he saw what had upset Annie so much. But once Leo got past the initial verbalization of his wish, it should be all right. There wouldn't be any more need to dodge the issue.

Feeling guilty had become something he was living with, and this was adding one more to the pile. He was a little wary as Annie approached. His mind switched like a radio station to the kiss, and his head filled with static as he fought the memory off. This was no time to be thinking about how it had turned his world upside down.

"Hi, guys," she said, resting her hand on Leo's shoulder. "What in the world have you been up to?" She laughed when he grinned through his milk mustache.

"I got us fellas a snack."

"I can see that. I'm sure Colt and Luke appreciated that very much."

She was acting as if nothing had happened between them. He got the feeling Montana and Gabi knew some of what had transpired, and that it was part of the reason Annie had gone off with them. He was pretty sure they thought he was messing up, just as Luke and Annie did.

But Colt had to do what he had to do.

There just wasn't any way around that. Unless God reached down and lifted the burdens weighing on him, this was the way it was going to be.

"Okay, so it's all set," Gabi said, scooting close to Colt and rubbing elbows with him. "You're picking Annie and Leo up for the wedding. They can come early with you, because I'd like them in the pictures."

Colt rubbed the back of his neck, feeling pricks of apprehension. "Sure. If Annie's good with that, then that's what I'll do."

Annie smiled, her eyes twinkling so bright it had him wondering what had happened to the red-hot fury of a few hours ago.

"It sounds great to me. We're in, aren't we, Leo?"

Leo held up his hand to Colt for a high-five slap. "Great!"

Colt slapped his hand and couldn't help but wonder if he was missing something…something important.

Chapter Sixteen

Saturday arrived quicker than Annie realized. She'd been telling herself since Thursday that everything was going to work out. Ha! She had the notorious matchmaking posse of Mule Hollow plotting and praying behind her back. She had a little boy dreaming and wishing his hero was his daddy—who actually *was* his daddy. She had his aunts and uncles praying, too.

At this point, with all the tangled and twisted emotions rousting about inside her, Annie wasn't sure what she needed—or wanted—to pray for. Did she want to be a match made in Mule Hollow? Could she trust her heart to someone when the fear of rejection clung so closely to her? When she'd driven into town just a few short weeks ago, the answer to that question would have been a resounding no.

Especially someone like Colt, who had such severe emotional scars himself.

Now… Now she wasn't so sure. The time she'd spent being included in the family drew her even more than the attraction and love she felt for Colt.

For days she'd asked herself what it was about Colt

that would make her fall for the man. The answer had been easy. Despite his not wanting to tell Leo he was his daddy, she knew he loved him. She also loved his kindness. She loved his drive, his dedication. She loved the energy she felt when he looked at her and the kindness in his manner.

And deep down, when all was said and done, she knew that what was driving his desire not to tell Leo he was his daddy was the deep-rooted channel of hurt that ran through him. His kindness, his goodness and the way the tragedy of the wreck had affected him on such a deep level touched her. He needed to find a way to move forward and continue his life. But his ability to take responsibility the way he did struck a chord within Annie. In all her life, that decent willingness to take responsibility had been missing.

If he could, in time, surpass all of that and claim his son…she might be able to risk her heart. If not, the matchmakers were in for a disappointing ending to their new plan.

"You are looking mighty handsome." She straightened Leo's long-sleeved white dress shirt. He'd done his best to get the tails tucked in, but they were crooked all the way around. Annie made quick work of the task and used it as an excuse to fuss over him. She gave him a quick hug and a kiss on the cheek. "Do you know how much I love you?"

He opened his arms wide. "More than this, you said last time. But I've grown since then."

"And I still love you more than that. Your arms can never grow longer than my love."

"And your arms can never grow longer than my love."

He pecked her on the cheek, and she very nearly started blubbering all over his white shirt.

"You know your momma would have been so proud of you, don't you?"

He looked thoughtful. "I bet she would like that Colt is teaching me how to be a cowboy. My momma sure did love bull riding. And Colt, too. I've been thinking about that a lot lately."

Annie wasn't so sure Jennifer would have been happy about her having brought Leo and Colt together. But she wasn't going to tell Leo that. Instead, she smiled. "She would have loved that you were having a good time."

The sound of a truck coming to a halt in the drive alerted them both that Colt had arrived. Annie straightened her dress. She'd dug through her clothes and found a pale mint-green dress that someone had given her after the fire. It was a slim design and fit her very well, the hem resting just at her knees. Annie paired it with two-inch sandals that she found in the box of shoes she'd been given.

One day she'd go to the store and actually buy some of her own clothing, but there was no hurry. She felt such a sense of gratitude for the generosity of all those who'd rushed to her aid and that of the other residents who'd been burned out of their homes. She smoothed a hand over the front of her dress and checked her makeup in the hall mirror…it was good to make sure she looked her best for the wedding. The fact that Colt happened to be seeing her first—well, she couldn't help that.

"You sound ridiculous," she muttered as she took a deep breath. She was going to behave herself, and she certainly wasn't going to provoke a kiss. There was no denying that he felt the chemistry that surged between them. But whether his emotions were engaged like hers was still a mystery to her.

Leo had the door open before Colt got to the steps. Racing outside, Leo threw himself off the edge of the porch and into Colt's arms. Thankfully, Colt caught the better part of Leo's weight with his good arm, and luckily his bad arm was almost fully healed. That had been apparent when she'd found him unloading hay on Thursday evening.

"Good catch," Leo bragged, holding his feet out so Colt could see his boots. "What do you think? Aunt Annie cleaned my boots all up and shined—and everything."

"Hey, those look almost brand-new. Matter of fact, I thought they were new."

"Nope, these were a gift from another little boy my age who gave them to me after the fire burned our house down. He wore 'em a little bit but when he heard about all us people's stuff burning up, he sent them to the donation place and I got them. Ain't that special? Annie Aunt—I mean, *Aunt Annie*—she told me how special that is 'cause that little kid was thinking about helping others and not just about how much he liked these cool boots."

Colt was still holding Leo on his hip, and though Leo was six years old, it was easy to see that Leo's size didn't make it a hardship on him. Leo was too big when it came to Annie trying to hold him anymore. She had to be content to sit in a big fluffy chair and cuddle while they read a book. Her days of toting him around were long gone.

After a quick exchange they loaded up into Colt's truck and snapped their seat belts into place.

"I've never been to a wedding before, Colt. Have you?"

"A few. I was usually on the road heading to a rodeo, though, since most of them happen on weekends."

Annie leaned back, content to listen to them talk. She slid a glance at Colt as he focused on the road. He wore black dress jeans paired with a buff-colored Western shirt that looked great with his sandstone-colored hair and his warm brown eyes. His Stetson was a similar color. The man looked good, no question about it.

"So I guess we just get there early and they start taking pictures?" She knew he was making small talk to fill in the silence hanging between them. He'd been instructed very clearly about what the schedule was upon their arrival.

"That's it," she said, going along with him. The best thing would be for Leo to start chattering away again, and then they wouldn't have to have any conversation at all.

But Leo was busy looking out the window, his brow etched in deep thought. She was surprised that he hadn't told Colt that he wished he was his daddy. Annie wasn't sure if that would be a good thing or a bad thing. But she'd decided she'd stay out of it and let whatever Leo decided to say to his daddy be completely natural. With no interference from her end.

"Aunt Annie and Colt. I been thinking," he said unexpectedly. "I think we feel like a family."

Annie was startled beyond belief. By the way Colt jerked the wheel, he got a kick in the gut from it, too.

Not done, Leo kept right on talking. "At day care yesterday I told Bobbie I wanted Colt to be my daddy, and he started laughing at me. I told him that families come in all shapes now days—I heard that on the television. You could be the momma, Aunt Annie, and Colt could be the daddy. But that would make y'all married and Bobbie said that might be a problem. He said his momma and daddy didn't like each other and that's why his momma and him moved to Mule Hollow without his daddy. I told him y'all like each other. Well, y'all do," he clarified when he saw Annie's eyes grow wider. "So we could be a family."

Colt was the one who reacted first...a good thing, since Annie had no words at all. "Leo," he said. "It doesn't work exactly like that. But you hang in there, because one of these day your Aunt Annie's going to find someone to love and then you'll have your family."

Annie had never been so happy to see a little white church in all her life. Some men! Sometimes they just didn't have the sense God gave an ant. She shook her head in disgust at Colt and climbed out of the truck as fast as her two legs would carry her. Any other part of that conversation Colt wanted to have with his son, he could have it without her. It was either that or she was going to grab the man by the ear and twist until he told Leo what he wanted to hear—that he was his daddy, not that they were getting married!

Dear Lord, keep me from violence, Annie silently chanted all the way to the front door of the church to the rhythm of her stomps. Distance—that was what she needed and she needed it now.

* * *

Annie had calmed down by the time the wedding took place. It was a beautiful ceremony and Leo didn't ask her during the exchange of vows about her and Colt getting married again. He waited until the newlyweds were kissing. Tugging on her shirtsleeve, he looked up at her. "I bet you'd have fun doin' that with Colt. I think if he can ride a bull good like he does, then he can make himself be good at anything. Even bein' a good kisser."

The sound of chuckles rippling around her told Annie that there were plenty of ears who'd heard Leo's observation. Leo didn't know just how good of a kisser Colt was.

The night was still young and Leo was on a roll. Annie was a little terrified as she watched a glowing Gabi and Jess walk down the aisle and out the door. Annie wasn't sure if she was going to make it through many more of Leo's outbursts.

But what could she say? Nothing. Absolutely nothing. Where Colt was concerned her lips were sealed.

"Colt, you looked sourer than ol' Applegate standin' up thar next to yor brothers," Sam said, coming over to where Colt was standing alone, drinking pink punch in a dainty glass cup. He almost didn't pick up the drink because he didn't want to be caught holding such a thing, but he needed to drink something, even if it was pink punch in a punch cup.

"Sam. And good evening to you, too." The music was playing and Colt had been watching couples dance past him, two-stepping to some good country music. He was guzzling punch because his throat kept getting dry every time he looked across the dance floor and saw Annie help serve the cake.

He hadn't been able to stop thinking about what Leo had said in the truck on the way to the wedding. And then there was that last kiss they'd had...he hadn't meant to grab her up and kiss her like that. It had been out of his control from the moment he'd reached for her. Annie Ridgeway ignited emotions in him that shook him up. And then there was his son. Dreaming of a family.

It had taken everything in him not to blurt out the truth.

But he'd remained firm and held out revealing the truth...the *truth*. He understood what Annie meant by being compromised. It felt as though he'd been lying to Leo, but he'd actually managed to word his answer so that he hadn't lied. But was that fair to Annie or to Leo?

Esther Mae came from out of nowhere and was standing beside him. "You do know you can ask a girl to dance."

"Why, Esther Mae," he said, forcing his bad mood into the shadows. The woman's erratically colored dress was enough to shock the doldrums out of the worst-case scenarios. "I'm flattered that you want to dance with me, but what's Hank going to say?"

Esther Mae pushed on his arm and turned a tinge of pink. "He's gonna be just fine with it." A mischievous twinkle lit her eyes. "It'll be good for him."

Not really wanting to dance, but not willing to tell Esther Mae no, Colt took Esther's hand and led her onto the dance floor. Allan Jackson had just begun singing a perfect two-step song. When Colt spun Esther so they moved across the dance floor in one direction, she spun them right back—so she was pretty much leading.

"Sorry," she said. "I'm not one on dancing backwards."

They were battling it out over who was leading and who wasn't when Hank and Annie danced by. Colt hadn't seen her dance all night. Just like him, she'd stayed off the dance floor, but here she was, one hand on Hank's shoulder and the other hand slipped into his.

"Well, there goes my Hank," Esther Mae huffed. "That man hasn't asked me to dance all night long and here he is with Annie."

Colt knew a setup when he saw it. He wasn't one to mess up their fun, and he couldn't help himself; he wanted to dance with Annie. He spun Esther Mae in the direction of Hank. He was going to help this setup along.

Annie had been surprised when Hank had asked her to dance. There had been no way she was going to tell the nice man no. He'd always been kind to Leo and she appreciated that very much.

"Well, look, there is my Esther Mae." He stopped suddenly beside Colt and Esther Mae. "Do you mind?" he said, then grinned at Colt. "May I cut in?"

Esther Mae grinned. "Oh, honey, that is so sweet. Do you mind?" she asked Colt as she was already reaching for her husband's hand. Colt and Annie were standing in the middle of the dance floor, leaving Annie feeling a little silly when Colt didn't ask her to continue the dance with him. She turned to walk off and he snagged her hand and whirled her around into his arms.

Annie gasped as one arm came around her, tugging

her close, and the other held her hand near his heart as he began leading her to the music.

"I didn't mean to keep you standing there. It just stunned me for a minute."

Her heart was pounding so furiously that she was certain he could feel it in the small space between them. "I—" she started, trying to catch her breath. "I wasn't sure you cared to dance with me."

"I care."

His words were so short and so straightforward they caught her off guard and she stepped on his toe. "Sorry."

"Any time." His lips curved into a slow smile and his eyes were steady—full of unreadable emotions.

Oh, how she wished she could read what was going through his mind.

They danced to the music and Annie tried not to let it mean anything. It was just a dance. A dance they'd been conned into dancing together. It did not mean anything.

I care.

His words echoed through the distance she was struggling to keep between Colt and her heart.

"About what Leo said…" he said finally, pulling Annie back from inside her head.

"Which part?" There were so many different things he'd said in such a short time.

Colt spun her almost as if it were an automatic response to the beat of the music. It was apparent that he'd danced much more than she had. It was a reminder of his life on the road.

"Yeah, he said a lot, didn't he?"

The music wound to an end. They were standing on the edge of the dance floor. Hay bales were stacked at various places for decorations and seating. Plants and an array of baskets also added a charm and warmth to the barn. Colt released her, dropping his hands and tucking them into his pockets as if not knowing what to do with them now.

They were near a fairly large decorated area, offering some seclusion. She nodded—what could she say? Leo's argument went on and on: *We could be a family. Colt could be my daddy. Y'all like each other...* His little mind churned overtime. It saddened Annie. "You need to tell him you're his daddy, Colt. He's talking about wanting you to be his daddy and has no idea that you really are his daddy."

"I can't do it."

"I know you don't *want* to. That you'd rather it go on like this, but I can't lie to him anymore. I can't continue to let him think you are just a man he admires. Whether you want it that way or not, he has a right to know." Annie raised her hands in surrender. "You figure this out," she said, frustrated beyond words by the look of denial still shimmering in Colt's eyes. What was wrong with this man? "I need to go check on Leo. It's been a little while since I spotted him."

She needed to get away from Colt and she really did need to check on Leo. He'd been running around the reception with the other kids, but as she glanced around she didn't see him.

"I'll help." Colt followed her.

Annie wanted to scream but held her tongue. Instead she stayed a step ahead of him so she wouldn't have to look at him. When they didn't find Leo in the building, they went outside. There was a smaller building not too far away and they headed that direction. The farther away from the music they got, the sound of puppies yapping could be heard. Colt and Annie's eyes met, understanding that this could very well be where he was, since he loved puppies.

Sure enough, they found him sitting on a bale of hay surrounded by six not-yet-weaned puppies. Instead of smiling and playing with them happily, tears stained Leo's face when he looked up at them.

"Hey, little buddy," Colt said. "What's the matter?"

"Annie Aunt, he's my daddy," Leo said, ignoring Colt, his lip trembling and a big tear rolling down his cheek. "And he don't want me."

The words weren't a question but a sad statement.

And it broke Annie's heart.

Chapter Seventeen

"No, Leo," Colt gasped, kneeling in front of his son, tears springing to his eyes. "I want you. I never meant it like that. I just had something very bad happen and it messed my thinking up. I was going to tell you I was your daddy as soon as I..." Colt's heart was breaking. Seeing the pain in Leo's eyes tore at him. He thought of all the children out there whose lives were messed up by parents who didn't want them or couldn't take care of them. He couldn't believe he'd even hesitated in telling Leo that he was his daddy. What had he been thinking?

"Leo, I love you, son. Can you forgive me?"

Leo was breathing hard through his tears as a smile, slow and hesitant, spread across his face. "You're my daddy. I can only love you."

Emotions so strong overtook Colt, and he was glad he was already kneeling or his knees might have buckled. He wrapped his arms around Leo and hugged him close. Their first hug as father and son. This was the beginning of their future. The magnitude of it all filled Colt and he gladly took on the magnificent burden, though he still felt unworthy of the blessing. *Thank you, God.*

Looking up, he found Annie crying. "Thank you," he mouthed the words. She smiled, wiping the tears with her fingertips.

Leo raised his head and grinned. "See, that ol' Bobbie, he don't know nothin'. I was right all along. If you're my daddy then you and Annie Aunt can get married and we really *can* be a family!"

Annie groaned. "Leo, you enjoy having your daddy, okay. I like things just the way they are."

Helping to redirect Leo's train of thought, Colt stood. "Come on, son, I think it's time to head home and let you get some rest. It's been a long day for you."

"Aw, Colt…" Leo paused. "Colt, can I call you… Daddy?"

Colt nodded. There was going to be some explaining to do around town, but he had no doubt that word would spread like wildfire. Looking at Leo, pride filled him.

He grinned. "Only if I can call you Son. How does that sound?"

"It sounds great!"

Now that he knows, what's next? Annie listened to the distant call of a lone coyote and tried not to picture herself being that lonely. Long after Colt had dropped them off and headed to his house, Leo had continued talking about his daddy.

And why shouldn't he? He had every right to be excited. On the way home from the wedding, she'd finally had to tell him that Colt had his home and they had their home, and they would not be getting married and moving in together. It was embarrassing—thankfully, he hadn't known how his excitement was affecting her.

Colt was uncomfortable about it, too, but she'd been the one who'd addressed it.

And that was the way she wanted it. She surely didn't want the cowboy thinking she wanted to get married. Not because of Leo, anyway.

That being the case, she realized that she needed to face reality. There was a possibility that Leo might not want to continue to live with her. The thought put a catch in her heart. The reality was that Colt was Leo's daddy, and he very well might want his son living with him. Her role stood a small chance of becoming that of the traditional aunt.... It was something she'd known might be a reality, so she'd cloaked the thought in heavy cover and not let herself peek at it until now.

What was she going to do?

Pacing the porch, she tried to shake off the chill that gripped her despite the temperature hovering in the eighties, even at midnight.

She was going to hit this nail on the head with a hard hammer. *That is what I am going to do.*

"Colt," she said out loud, for only the lonely coyote to hear, if he happened to be listening. "I think Leo is right. We should be a family. Why? Funny you should ask, because I love you and..."

Grabbing hold of the porch pole, she rested her head against the smooth wood and took a deep breath. Just because a man kissed her, was the daddy of the child she loved and made her feel like she was going to suffocate when he looked at her, it wasn't a reason to fall in love. The suffocating part was plenty of reason to run. But here she was thinking... "Thinking's going to get you in trouble," she muttered, and slapped the pole.

"You're going to get splinters in your forehead if you keep that up." Colt's warm, husky voice caused Annie to jump.

"Don't *do* that!" she exclaimed, glaring at him as he moved with stealthy grace the last few feet to where she stood.

Her forehead stung and she rubbed the spot. "What are you doing?"

He shrugged. "Couldn't sleep. Just like you. I think we need to talk—without Leo controlling the conversation."

Boy, was that an understatement. "I couldn't agree more."

She'd been cold before but now she felt the heat of the night dampening the edges of her hairline. Colt had changed into a T-shirt and well-worn jeans. He was also hatless, his hair a mess, as if he'd worried it to death as he'd traipsed across the pastures. Behind him, a flash of lightning splintered across the sky and two beats later thunder cracked, threatening that the heavens were about to split wide open.

"That tore me up today, Annie."

She nodded at his quiet words. "Me, too."

"My childhood haunts me, Annie."

"Mine, too." She took a deep breath, her nerves settling a bit as she forced herself to focus on Leo and not on the way Colt stirred up her emotions. "I want so badly for Leo to know the love of—" Her words broke off. If she said what she wished for more than anything, it would be that she really wanted the three of them to be a family, just like Leo kept going on about. However, that would be saying too much.

"I want him to have more than I had," Colt said, moving to stand closer to her. His eyes were almost black in the moonlight. "I want him to know the love and security of a family."

"I do, too—I want that so much," Annie blurted before being able to stop herself. "But having us both love him, and having us living so close, is going to work so much better than before. He's going to have security... and then there's your family. All living here right close," she rambled on, the intensity of Colt's expression rattling her. "I wish there was more we could do—I don't know what, though."

"Marry me."

Annie's heart stopped. The breath in her lungs slipped away.

"Excuse me?" she gasped at last, her heart kicking in with a vengeance.

Colt grabbed her by the arms. "Marry me, Annie. We can give Leo everything you said. We can do this for Leo. I've thought about it, Annie. I used to think I didn't want a family—after my childhood. I just didn't have a desire for one. Leo has changed all of that and I honestly never knew I could love someone like this. We could give him a good life. We could make a home life like we both missed out on. We both love him—this would be the best."

Annie's eyes narrowed. Her heart chilled. She pulled one arm, then the other from Colt's easy grasp, and she took a step back from him.

He wasn't asking her to marry him because he felt anything for her. It was for Leo.

It was for practical purposes.

Traitorous heart that she had, she was tempted to say yes just to be close to him. Couldn't Colt loving Leo be enough? Couldn't living in one household be enough?

She would not cry. She would *not* cry... She blinked hard. "I—" she said, the word croaking from her like a frog with a bad cold. "I need to think about this."

"I know there should be more, Annie. But this is all I can give."

Those words cut deeper than anything he'd said. Love wasn't something to be controlled, she'd learned. She'd thought she could do it by putting up shields around her own heart, yet it had happened despite all the shields and fear.

It had happened to her, and sadly hadn't happened to Colt.

"I understand," she said, keeping her own heart's secret closely hidden. She forced a smile she didn't feel. "I'll let you know soon. For Leo's sake."

Looking as if he had more to say, he remained silent, nodded, then turned and walked away. Lightning cracked in the distance and the thunder boomed.

"Do you need a ride?" Annie called, even though riding with him right now was not where she wanted to be. Distance and time. That was what she needed.

"I'm fine. I want the walk. Good night, Annie."

She wondered how it was that he'd hurt her so, and yet watching him go, she felt as though she'd hurt *him*. Had he really, really expected her to say yes on the spot to his marriage of convenience? Because that was exactly what he'd just proposed. Funny how in movies and books it always seemed like such a romantic kind of setup.

Reality was not fiction, though. Annie's heart ached

and no romanticism in the world could make it feel better. She prayed that with time God would heal her heart—for Leo's sake.

Colt knew he'd hurt Annie. It had been clearly written in her eyes the moment he'd explained his proposition. Oh, clearer than that he'd recognized the joy—disbelief—but joy, that illuminated those gorgeous pale eyes of hers when he'd first said, "Marry me."

Like the clashing emotions warring inside him, the distant storm rolled in fast. He'd gotten halfway between his place and Annie's when the skies opened up and a furious downpour hit.

Colt was drenched before he could look for cover. It didn't matter anyway; he knew better than anyone there was none in either direction, except his house and Annie's....

Quickening his step, he ducked his head against the pelting rain. Rain that was blowing sideways because the wind was so violent.

Less than a hundred feet away lightning cut through the sky and struck a tree. Colt saw the explosion and felt the sizzle beneath his feet the same instant he was blown into the air....

Annie stared through the pouring rain. Colt hadn't been gone long when the sky opened up. For months, Texas had suffered and shriveled up from lack of water, and of all times for God to decide to bless them with a flood!

Sometimes she had to wonder what He was thinking! Of course, Colt was the one who'd walked across the pasture in the dead of night while thunder rolled in the background. Despite not having had rain for ages and ages, Texas weather was unpredictable.

Maddening as he was, she was worried silly about him. When the distant sky ignited after a lightning bolt struck something, Annie couldn't stand it any longer. Colt could not have made it home before that had happened. Giving up, she hurried to check on Leo. He was sleeping right through the storm—unbelievable, but good. She grabbed her raincoat and car keys and headed out after Colt.

Her car was not a truck. That became apparent within the first few feet. The parched earth's lack of moisture, combined with more areas of dried-up grass with no roots to hold the dirt in place, did not play well with the enormous amount of water rushing from the sky. Why, in the twenty minutes she'd wasted deciding whether to go after Colt, ruts and mud holes had appeared that threatened to bog her down. Or worse, sweep her off the disappearing gravel road completely.

Her heart was thundering harder than the thunder and her pulse was more erratic than the lightning. *Please, God, let him be okay.*

Lightning flashed and lit up the night. She saw him. He was half up on his knees, as if he'd just been thrown from a bull and was disoriented as he struggled to gain his feet.

Not far away was a huge oak tree split down the middle by a mighty bolt of lightning. Even in the rain it sizzled, and smoke rose up from the fire that burned in the splayed open portions of trunk.

Annie slammed on her brakes. The car slid and came

to a halt not far from Colt. By the time she got out of the clunker and made it to him, he'd stumbled to his feet. She grabbed him around the waist and held on when it seemed as if he might fall back down. Annie was praying fiercely. "I'm here, Colt. Hold on."

"What are you doing here?" he demanded, even as he struggled. Rain poured down on them like a waterfall.

"I'm here to help you, you big goof."

He chuckled. "You know you came because you love me."

"That lightning messed you up, didn't it?" she stated as they headed toward her car. As if to acknowledge that it could do more, the sky lit up once more. Annie jumped and Colt's arm tightened around her.

"It's not that bad. I've been thrown off bulls that hurt worse." His voice held a cocky grin that sent shivers of gladness through Annie.

"I'm sure you have. But I haven't, so let's hurry!"

By the time they reached the car, Colt wasn't as stunned—a fact that had her feeling better about the whole situation. Once he was inside, she raced around to the driver's side, slipping and falling in a mud hole face-first!

"I'm fine." She sputtered mud as Colt moved from the safety of the car to help her. Grasping her by the arms, he pulled her up out of the mud. "Sure you are, but we're in this together."

To Annie's surprise, Colt swung her up into his arms and carried her to the passenger side of the car. Apparently, there were no life-threatening injuries to the man.

After depositing her into the seat, he gave her a swift kiss on her muddy lips. "Thanks for coming to my rescue," he said, then closed the door and hurried around the car. Thankfully, he was safely inside once again within seconds.

"You okay?" he asked, taking hold of the steering wheel.

"Y-yes." Her teeth chattered despite the warmth of the night. There was a chill in the air from the storm. "Are you?"

"I am now. There's nothing like a lightning bolt to clear a man's head."

Annie groaned. "Only a daredevil like you would think that."

Colt reached for her hand. "Not *think*. Know. Annie, please hear me out. I've been so torn up over the death of the Eversons and my part in their deaths. No..." He placed a hand gently over her lips when she'd started to protest. "No. It doesn't matter how many times everyone tells me it wasn't my fault. I know in my heart that, even if it wasn't, I was too worn out to have helped prevent it if there had been the slightest window of opportunity. That fact alone will always be with me. That, plus the fact that I can't remember the moments before the impact, will always make me wonder if I was asleep when I was hit. Or if I simply blanked out the trauma of the event. Unless I remember one day, which the doctor tells me I most likely won't, then it's a question I will go to my grave wondering."

"I understand." Finally knowing it was true, Annie felt some of the heavy burden of responsibility he would always carry.

"I've struggled with the ability to feel joy. The guilt when I look at Leo has, at times, torn me down. I'm not worthy of the gift of that child, and yet he's mine. Even though God knows I'm not worth one strand on that little boy's head, He gave him to me anyway… It's just like—"

"Grace and forgiveness," Annie said, seeing the truth.

"Yes. I'm still not worthy of that, but God gave it to us. But Annie, I was laid out in that mud, stunned and unable to move from the jolt of electricity that had traveled through my body. While I was sprawled there realizing I was still alive, I thought only of you."

Annie's heart dared to hope.

"I love you, Annie. I just wouldn't let myself feel it. Or admit it. How could I deserve Leo? And then you, too? I don't know why I'm still here, but when I was lying there, I started praying that you loved me, too. Do you…?"

Annie stopped his question with a kiss—mud and all. Lightning flashed and thunder boomed and Annie couldn't have cared less. She was in the arms of the man she loved. And the man who loved her.

"I guess that's a yes?" Colt asked when she turned him loose.

She chuckled. "For a bull rider, you're one smart cowboy."

"I'm one blessed cowboy, undeserving as anyone and yet blessed beyond comprehension."

A lump lodged in her throat. "I love you, Colt Holden. I really do."

With a tender look in his eyes, he pulled her close and kissed her. "Then marry me like I asked earlier… except, know that it will be so that we can make a home full of love for all of us."

Annie could only nod, her heart was so full. Colt

smiled in understanding. He touched her cheek, his fingers warm as they trailed across her skin.

"I love you," she said at last. "Always."

His eyes darkened with emotion. "I like the sound of that."

"I do, too."

They smiled at each other.

"Then, future Mrs. Colt Holden, let's get this boat turned toward home and tell our boy."

Annie closed her eyes and let the sensation fill her with all the joy she could handle. "Lead the way, cowboy—I'm here for the full eight-second ride and beyond."

Colt chuckled and pressed the gas pedal. The car bolted forward. "That's my girl. I knew you were going to come to love my sport." He grinned. "Just wait till I tell Leo."

His girl. She liked the sound of that very, very much....

Epilogue

Colt straightened his hat and stared at his reflection in the mirror of Luke's guest bedroom. Behind him the door slid open, letting in the laugher and chatter from the other side.

"You nervous, little brother?" Jess asked as he and Luke entered the room.

"I've never been more nervous. My adrenaline levels are sky-high."

"It's normal to feel scared right before you walk down the aisle." Luke grinned, his tone teasing.

"I didn't say I was scared. I'm rarin' and ready to get this chute opened and start life with Annie and Leo."

In the two weeks since he'd asked her to marry him, Colt's life had changed in many ways. Sheriff Brady had called him the day after Annie had agreed to marry him. He'd ask if Colt had ever thought about speaking splayed open about the wreck with the drunk driver. They'd talked and Colt had realized that he could make a positive change in someone's life if he shared how the wreck had affected him. Especially the impact of his lack of sleep and the responsibility a person bore when he not only got behind the wheel while intoxicated, but also when he got behind the wheel in a state of sleep deprivation. It was a positive step and one he felt God was leading him to take. If he could help save one life…there could be some good brought from the bad. The thought gave him hope and a feeling of satisfaction that he could help make a difference. And it would be at least some small way of redeeming his own bad judgment.

He was moving forward, and he was full of excitement and hope and the joy for what lay ahead for him, Annie and Leo. God's goodness stunned him, and he would never forget that.

Colt turned back to the mirror and his brothers stepped up to stand beside him. Luke laid an arm across Colt's and Jess's shoulders, meeting their eyes in the mirror. "I'm proud to call you brothers. Proud to see the men you've become."

Colt met Jess's eyes, and they knew their older brother's acceptance of responsibility too big for his young shoulders had led them in their faith, and into becoming the kind of men they wanted to be.

"You know we have a long way to go to live up to the standards you've set," Jess said, a teasing light twinkling in his eyes.

"Yeah," Colt added with a chuckle that felt good. "We know you're just glad we're about to fill this ranch with all kinds of kids, just like you wanted the day you talked us into throwin' in with you on buying it."

"Hey, in that case, let's get this wedding going and then let's get busy."

Three sets of eyebrows cocked and matching grins followed.

The door opened behind them and Leo peeked inside. Behind him Norma Sue could be heard.

"Take your seats, everyone," she ordered. "That means you, App. Turn on your hearing aid and sit down so we can get this show on the road."

"Norma Sue, I ain't never seen a more bossy woman in all my days—"

"App, I'm warning you."

Leo's eyes were wide as he closed the door. "I think Norma Sue's gonna hog-tie Mr. Applegate. He said she was just mad 'cause you and my Aunt Annie was gettin' hitched and her and her posse didn't have nothin' to do with it."

When Colt, Luke and Jess all laughed, Leo looked perplexed. "Esther Mae said it didn't matter if they did or didn't as long as y'all were tyin' the knot. She said they had made some plans, but God beat them to it when He struck you down with a lightn' bolt to the heart."

Colt picked his son up and hugged him. "She'd be right about that. And I agree one hundred percent. As long as I get you and your sweet aunt, I don't care who matched me up."

Leo grinned and threw his arms around Colt's neck. "Me, too."

A rap on the door had Luke pulling it open. "Yoo-hoo," Esther Mae called, sticking her head around inside. "Are y'all ready? Norma Sue's about to bust a gut to get you and Annie married." Her eyes twinkled.

"Me, too. I'm bustin' a gut, too," Leo agreed. Wiggling out of Colt's arms, he took his hand. "Come on, Daddy, let's do this."

"Lead the way, son."

With Leo leading his daddy and his uncles, they filed out of the bedroom and into the large den to stand beside the preacher in front of the large window overlooking the ranch. Chance had been thrilled when he'd heard all the good news. It had spread faster than even Colt had suspected it would. This was a small wedding with a large reception to follow. Still, the room was filled with people who were the family Colt, Luke and Jess had never had.

A smiling Adela began playing the music and the door opened. First Montana, then Gabi walked up the aisle to stand across from their husbands. Colt's heart was beating fast as Annie entered the room. She wore a simple white dress and stole his breath when her eyes met his and she smiled. Colt knew in that single moment in time that he'd come full circle. He'd been made by God to be Annie Ridgeway's husband. And Leo's daddy.

"Wow," Leo gasped, tugging on Colt's pant leg.

"The most beautiful girl in the world," Colt said, squeezing Leo's shoulder. *And she's mine*. He didn't deserve any of it, but God had given it to him anyway.

"Hey, cowboy," Annie whispered as she stood before him. "Are you ready?"

"Oh, yeah. I thought you'd never get here."

Leo cocked his head to the side, his eyes wide with dismay as he added in a loud whisper that filled the room. "And Norma Sue's gut is about to bust wide open, so Mr. Applegate said we better get this show on the road or it ain't gonna be pretty at all!"

"Well." Esther Mae chuckled. "For once App and I agree. Let's get this show on the road, because the last thing any of us need is for Norma Sue to bust—"

"Esther Mae," Norma Sue snapped. "Would you please let the preacher marry these two!"

App grunted, the room chuckled and Leo beamed broadly at his daddy and his sweet Annie Aunt. "Yeah, let's do this. I think guts are cool but this is gonna be a whole lot more fun!"

Colt and Annie's eyes held. They were in total agreement—the fun was just getting started....

* * * * *

If you enjoyed Debra Clopton's book, be sure to check out the other books this month from Love Inspired!

Dear Reader,

I am so happy you chose to spend time with me and the Mule Hollow gang! I hope, as I always hope, that your visit was a relaxing one, and that you'll come back again very soon.

In this, the last book of the Mule Hollow Homecoming series, Colt has lived through a tragedy that grieves his soul. There seems to be no hope for him through his own eyes because he can't forgive himself. Grace is the most beautiful gift in the world, and I loved writing Colt's journey back to healing and love. I hope you enjoyed meeting Annie and Leo.

I loved telling the Holden brothers' stories and hope if you haven't read Luke's and Jess's stories that you'll pick up copies of *Her Rodeo Cowboy* and *Her Lone Star Cowboy* to find out the rest of the story.

I'm busy, busy creating new stories—please drop by my new website from time to time at debraclopton.com, where I'll keep you updated on what's coming next! I love hearing from readers, either via my website or at P.O. Box 1125, Madisonville, TX 77864.

Until next time live, laugh and seek God with all your heart.

Debra Clopton

Questions for Discussion

1. Annie Ridgeway is on a mission to reveal to her nephew's father that he is a father. Why did Colt Holden not know he'd fathered a child?

2. When Annie meets Colt, she decides telling him right away might not be the best thing. Why does she decide to wait? What would you have done in her place?

3. Annie and her sister are very different women. Annie steered away from relationships, while Jennifer sought out casual connections with no strings attached. What part do you believe their backgrounds played in their behavior as adults?

4. When Colt's brothers try to help him move on from his grief, Colt gets angry and storms off. Why do you think he was angry at his brothers? Were they acting only out of love and concern?

5. Struggling to recover after the car accident, Colt feels guilty for the family's deaths because he feels he was too tired to be behind the wheel. Would you feel the same if you were in Colt's place? Why or why not?

6. The place that Annie rents for herself and Leo happens to be connected to Colt's back pasture. Is this a coincidence, or do you see God's hand in it? Explain.

7. Leo, Colt and Annie start spending a lot of time together, and Annie starts to have feelings for Colt. Was this a surprise to you, or did you see this coming? Please explain.

8. Both Colt and Annie had less than perfect childhoods. Could this be a reason they understand each other so well? Why or why not?

9. Colt is proud as can be when Leo takes an interest in riding bulls and other rodeo activities, even as Annie is extremely worried about it. Have you ever had to deal with a child or family member wanting to do something dangerous? How did you react?

10. Colt decides to create a ministry to use his experience in the car accident to help others and save lives. Have you or anyone you've known ever taken a bad experience and turned it into something positive? Share with the group how this was done.

REQUEST YOUR FREE BOOKS!

2 FREE INSPIRATIONAL NOVELS
PLUS 2
FREE
MYSTERY GIFTS

YES! Please send me 2 FREE Love Inspired® novels and my 2 FREE mystery gifts (gifts are worth about $10). After receiving them, if I don't wish to receive any more books, I can return the shipping statement marked "cancel." If I don't cancel, I will receive 6 brand-new novels every month and be billed just $4.49 per book in the U.S. or $4.99 per book in Canada. That's a saving of at least 22% off the cover price. It's quite a bargain! Shipping and handling is just 50¢ per book in the U.S. and 75¢ per book in Canada.* I understand that accepting the 2 free books and gifts places me under no obligation to buy anything. I can always return a shipment and cancel at any time. Even if I never buy another book, the two free books and gifts are mine to keep forever.

105/305 IDN FEGR

Name _____ (PLEASE PRINT)

Address _____ Apt. #

City _____ State/Prov. _____ Zip/Postal Code

Signature (if under 18, a parent or guardian must sign)

LIREG11B